More fantastically funny books by Stephen and Anita Mangan

Escape the Rooms
The Fart that Changed the World
The Unlikely Rise of Harry Sponge
The Great Reindeer Rescue
The Day I Fell Down the Toilet
The Fart that Broke World Book Day
The Fart that Saved the Universe

STEPHEN MANGAN

BARRIE SAVES CHRISTMAS

ILLUSTRATED BY
ANITA MANGAN

SCHOLASTIC

Published in the UK by Scholastic, 2025
Scholastic, Bosworth Avenue, Warwick, CV34 6UQ
Scholastic Ireland, 89E Lagan Road, Dublin Industrial Estate, Glasnevin, Dublin, D11 HP5F

SCHOLASTIC and associated logos are trademarks and/or
registered trademarks of Scholastic Inc.

Text © Stephen Mangan, 2025
Cover and inside illustrations © Anita Mangan, 2025

The moral rights of the author and illustrator have been asserted by them.

ISBN 978 0702 34417 6

A CIP catalogue record for this book is available from the British Library.

All rights reserved.
This book is sold subject to the condition that it shall not, by way of trade or otherwise,
be lent, hired out or otherwise circulated in any form of binding or cover other than
that in which it is published. No part of this publication may be reproduced, stored in a
retrieval system, or transmitted in any form or by any other means (electronic, mechanical,
photocopying, recording or otherwise), or used to train any artificial intelligence
technologies without prior written permission of Scholastic Limited. Subject to EU law,
Scholastic Limited expressly reserves this work from the text and data-mining exception.

Printed in the UK
Paper made from wood grown in sustainable forests and other controlled sources.

10 9 8 7 6 5 4 3 2

This is a work of fiction. Any resemblance to actual people, events or
locales is entirely coincidental.

The publisher does not have any control over and does not assume any
responsibility for any third-party websites or other platforms, or their content.

www.scholastic.co.uk

For safety or quality concerns:
UK: www.scholastic.co.uk/productinformation
EU: www.scholastic.ie/productinformation

To Mary, Carmel and all Irish grandparents everywhere

Chapter One
Barrie

Let me tell you a little bit about myself. I am a noble dog with a noble heritage, and good manners and dignity are at the very core of who I am.

When I meet some people for the first time, you can see them trying to work out whether I'm going to be a problem. Whether I'm going to be one of those angry, barky, aggressive types with no manners and no self-restraint. People put on fake smiles and try to look relaxed when they're not, and they say things like, **"Good boy!"** and **"There's a good boy!"** and **"Atta good boy!"** and **"My! You're a big fella!"**

If I run over to them and jump up to lick their faces to show them I'm friendly, that can be a problem too. In fact, it seems to make them even *more* nervous.

I'M JUST BEING FRIENDLY, GUYS.

Mrs Daniels from next door screamed and threatened to call the police the last time I tried to lick her face, so I got a big telling-off for that. And once I tried to lick the vicar's face when he stopped to talk to Dad at the front gate, and the vicar was so scared that he went bright red and left.

I may be big and look scary to some people, but I'm actually a big softie. I stay calm no matter how stressed everyone else is getting. I would never dream of hurting Laurence or Carrie and have looked after them since they were little babies. I always help people whenever I can – because I'm a type of dog that's been bred specifically to help people. I met another St Bernard years ago called Douglas and he told me everything. It's really interesting. Listen up.

There's a route over the mountains between Italy and Switzerland called the Great St Bernard Pass, named after a French guy called Bernard. It's an ancient route that has been used by humans for as long as humans have existed. And nearly a thousand years ago, right at the highest point of the road, where the wind howls fiercest and the snow piles deepest, some monks set up a shelter for travellers in need of rest or rescue. They called it the Great St Bernard Hospice because it was on the Great St Bernard Pass – which was named after that French bloke called Bernard, as I've said.

Lots of people would get lost while climbing up and down the mountains. They would lose track of the road, or fall into a deep pile of snow and not be

able to get out, or slip and hurt themselves and not be able to walk. The monks would try to help them. But it's hard looking for lost and hurt people in a snowstorm when you're a human and have no real sense of smell (sorry, humans – your sense of smell is rubbish), and often the monks going out to help hurt people would end up getting hurt themselves. So eventually a clever monk realized that what they needed were smart and strong dogs with a great sense of smell that didn't mind getting really,

really cold. The monks bred a type of dog to have all these qualities and they called these dogs St Bernards because the dogs belonged to the monks of the Great St Bernard Hospice, which was on the Great St Bernard Pass, which was named after the French bloke called Bernard, so it seemed like an appropriate name.

These St Bernard dogs were a huge success. This is how it worked…

Once the monks were told someone had gone missing or was hurt, two St Bernard dogs were sent out to look for them. They used their amazing sense of smell to find the missing people. Then one dog would run back to the hospice to fetch some monks and show them where to go, and the other dog would stay with the lost person. They were big dogs, so the person could cuddle up to them to get warm, and they also carried a little barrel around their necks with wine or brandy in it, so that the patient could have a drink while they waited for help to arrive.

Pretty clever, eh?

The St Bernards were never trained by the monks. The older dogs would teach the younger ones what to do. The skill and knowledge was passed along from dog to dog, from generation to generation.

So these brave and skilful dogs were my ancestors. I am proud to say I am a St Bernard.

And as I am a St *Bernard* from the St *Bernard* Hospice in the St *Bernard* Pass named after a bloke called *Bernard*, it's no surprise that my name is … Barrie.

Barrie?!

BARRIE?!

What were my humans thinking? Why wasn't

I Bernard? Or Bernie? It would have really suited me. **"Here comes good ol' Bernard the St Bernard,"** people would have said. **"Look, it's Big Bernie Bernard."**

Simple, easy to remember: Bernard.

But, no, I'm Barrie. Why? Because of a dad joke. LITERALLY. I was born just after Carrie. She's now nine. Her brother Laurence is ten. Dad said that sometimes people named Laurence get called Larry, so he thought it would be HILARIOUS if he had a son called Larry, a daughter called Carrie and a dog called Barrie.

So that was the name they gave me. Barrie.

Our surname is Barlow, so I'm Barrie Barlow. Pleased to meet you.

And, even though I'm called Barrie and not Bernard, I like to think my ancestors would approve of my dignity, my bravery and my sense of honour.

Chapter Two — Carrie

"Hey, Carrie. Do you think Barrie is the laziest dog on the planet?" Laurence asked me, munching on another chocolate from the big Christmas box Mum had given us. It was so big she'd given it to us *before* Christmas and we'd already eaten half of them.

"He's definitely the fartiest," I replied, wrinkling my nose. "Can't we feed him something that will help him be less ... gassy?"

"You know how fussy he is about his food, Carrie," said Laurence.

Laurence and I looked at Barrie lying there by

the fire, fast asleep. I loved that dog so much it hurt. He was, as far as I was concerned, just as much my brother as Laurence was. We had grown up together. We'd played together since as far back as I could remember. Like Mum and Dad and Laurence, Barrie had always been there.

Yes, he was lazy. Yes, he was farty. Yes, he

sometimes licked my face so hard he left gooey globules of dog saliva dripping down my cheeks. I didn't mind any of that. Apart from maybe the farty bit.

He must be dreaming, I thought as I watched him twitching in his sleep. What do St Bernards dream about? Bounding through the snow to rescue people? Braving the bone-chilling wind of a mountain blizzard? Every nerve straining, every muscle shaking with the effort, blotting out the desire to lie down and rest, knowing that if you did you might never get up again. Pushing yourself to the very edge of your limits and beyond. All to save the life of a stranger.

Barrie whimpered softly and his whole body shuddered. Laurence hummed and fidgeted too, constantly rearranging himself, legs bouncing, feet wiggling.

The funny thing was that Barrie didn't actually like the cold. He'd lie in front of the fire all day and all night if we let him. He didn't even like walks much.

Still, I loved him.

Chapter Three: Laurence

I bet I was annoying Carrie with my shuffling around, but I just couldn't get comfortable. The sofa always does this to me. One minute I'm fine, but then a second later the cushion behind me doesn't feel right, or the way my legs are arranged feels wrong and I have to shift to find a better position and – *wait, why don't I try lying down?* – so I put my head on the arm of the sofa, but that doesn't feel right either, so I sit up and pull my legs up to my chest to see if that helps.

It does for a second and then it doesn't, so I move again.

I know Carrie is used to me fidgeting like this, so maybe she doesn't even notice any more, but maybe she does notice and she hates it. She does things I hate too, though. Like the way she eats apples by crunching big chunks out of them *so noisily* and then chomping like a horse *so loudly* that I have to leave the room, or the way she taps her fingers on the kitchen table when she's doing her homework – *tap tap tap tap tap tap tap tap* – or the scratchy sound of her pen on the paper or—

Don't get me wrong. I like her and everything. She's kind and fun, and she tends to look on the bright side of most situations. Unlike me – I always think the worst is going to happen. But because she's my sister I'm around her a lot, so she tends to annoy me the most. And I'm sure I annoy her too. What if one day Carrie and Mum and Dad get so annoyed with me that they'll change the locks on the front door while I'm at school so I won't be able to get back into the house, and I'll stand there knocking on the front door for three hours, but they'll all be hiding from me under the kitchen table and Dad will be saying, **"I know this feels cruel, but it's best for everyone if Laurence goes off to live somewhere else because he annoys us and we annoy him and it'll never work, so just wait here quietly until he gets bored and goes away...?"** And eventually I'll give up knocking because it's obvious that they aren't going to let me in, and I'll walk sadly to the bus stop and get the first bus, which by chance takes me to the airport, where I get mistaken for a world-famous pilot who looks like me and, before I can object or before I know what's happening, I'm flying some Very Important People in a plane, but I'm not really a pilot, I'm just me, and the plane crashes, and at my funeral Mum and Dad and Carrie and Barrie are all sad, but they reckon it was probably for the best because I annoyed them and they annoyed me, but the thing is if they only stopped with the tapping and the crunching and the munching and the—

The door opened and Mum stuck her head round it and said, **"You two, we're out of mince pies. Can you go to the shop and get a pack, please? And take Barrie for a walk while you're at it. He hasn't been out today."**

So we do.

Chapter Four
Barrie

I didn't want to go for a walk. I was nice and cosy in front of the fire and it looked pretty wild and windy outside. But Mum stuck her head round the door and said something and then Carrie and Laurence jumped up, so I guess I ought to take them out. We St Bernards are famous for our loyalty and our service, after all. Still, I was having a nice dream about a squirrel.

I dream about this particular squirrel all the time. She's called Dorothea and she lives near us. I see her lolloping along the top of the wall at the end of our garden. She's always on the move, scurrying this way and that, doing goodness knows what. Which is fine – each to their own and everything – but quite often she'll stop and stare at me in a way that indicates she has *no respect*. Absolutely no respect at all. It's *my* garden, but she knows I can't get out if the back door is shut. She'll stare right at me like she's daring me to chase her, knowing I can't. And then she'll give a little smirk, as if to say, *You scared or what?*

When I was younger, that sort of thing would drive me wild with frustration and I'd bark and bark and bark, desperate to get out. But this seemed to annoy Mum and Dad and Laurence, or Carrie would start crying (this was when she was little), so after a while I learnt to control myself.

But you can't control your dreams and, most times when I'm asleep, Dorothea enters my dreams. She hops along the wall and she stands

there and she looks at me with that smirk, and in my dreams I open the back door (turn the key and everything) and slowly, because I am powerful and in control and dignified, I *walk* across our little back garden towards her. Dorothea is on the wall with that annoying expression on her face because she thinks I can't reach her up there, but in my dreams I jump – a mighty, spectacular, extraordinary jump – right up on to the wall, next to her, and you should see the look on Dorothea's face (this is always my favourite bit of the dream). The look of astonishment that a dog as strong and as large as me could jump that high.

There's always a brief pause at this point as we face off, while she works out what to do. That's when I say, **"I mean you no harm, Dorothea, but this is my wall, and if you're going to use it, then the least you can do is show me a bit of respect!"**

Dorothea turns and runs, and I follow. She twists and leaps and jumps this way and that, but I'm right behind her all the way because I am fast and nimble and just plain awesome.

The chase part of the dream can go on for a long time, and the strange thing is that, even though I am fast and nimble and just plain awesome, I never catch Dorothea. She always remains ahead as we streak across the city, over walls and fences, under cars, across parks. She's always a little bit further in front of me. That bushy tail, that squirrel scent, those little back legs always out of my reach.

Anyway, I was having this dream when Mum came in and woke me up. I should take the kids for a walk like she wants. Only, all of a sudden, it feels so warm inside and I think about how cold it is outside and I decide not to go for a walk, after all.

Chapter Five: Carrie

"Come on, Barrie! Walkies!"

His head jerked up and he looked at me. Then he laid his head right down again.

So lazy.

Laurence was already out in the hall getting his coat on.

Barrie's black, wet nose twitched. His snout is white, as are his front legs and chest, and then he has patches of almost black and lots more of brown. He's a handsome dog.

I grabbed him by the collar and tried to pull him to his feet, but he's way heavier than me so there was no way that was going to work. He's the heaviest member of our family. He's our protector, so it's right he should be big. Like a bouncer. Trouble is, I'm not sure Barrie knows quite how large he is. If you open the back door of the car, he'll leap in and try to sit on the back seat, but there isn't room for him to do that and he'll get stuck. Completely stuck. We have to go to the front passenger seat and move it forward so we can let him out.

Happens all the time. It's hilarious, but you'd think he'd have learnt by now.

"Come on, Barrie," I said again. **"Walkies!"**

He looked up with his big sad eyes and farted.

"Come on!" shouted Laurence from the hallway.

"Barrie won't get up!" I called back.

Laurence hates being made to wait, but I try to make it fun by finding something for him to do instead.

"Is Barrie's lead out there?" I asked, knowing full well that it was.

But Laurence was already one step ahead of me, and he came into the living room with the lead. I slipped out to the hallway to put my coat on and got some cash from Mum for the mince pies.

Chapter Six
Laurence

It's not like we haven't been for a walk with Barrie before – he goes for *two walks a day*. That's every single day. Two walks. So that's seven hundred and thirty walks a year, isn't it? Every year.

He knows the deal. He's done this before. He knows I'll put the lead on, and then we'll turn left out of the house, and he'll do a wee quite quickly once we're outside and maybe a poo a bit later, so we take poo bags with us to pick it up.

He has a bigger walk earlier in the day when

he gets to go to the park, but the evening walk is short and snappy. That's why Carrie and I do it. If we don't do one of the walks, Mum and Dad will moan about how they only got the dog for me and Carrie, so why are they having to do all the work, when – let's be real – I was a year old when we got Barrie, and Carrie was a new baby, so it's not like we asked them to get a dog. We couldn't even speak then, so how could we? Mind transfer? Baby magic? I don't think so. They can't blame it on us.

Don't get me wrong. I love Barrie – maybe more than I love anything else in the whole world, including my sister and my parents, but don't tell them that. And I like taking him for a walk even when it's cold out like today. I like checking out everyone's Christmas decorations.

I went into the living room with the lead.

Carrie went to put her coat on and Barrie was just lying there.

I attached the lead to his collar and said, **"Let's go, Barrie. Stop being lazy! You'll like it when you're out."**

He wasn't moving, so I pulled hard again on the lead, and that was when Barrie barked really loudly.

I know he'd never hurt me, but still I wasn't expecting him to bark. I jumped half out of my skin and my face went hot, and it was like there was a tidal wave of feeling rippling right through me and I felt suddenly angry.

I shouted, **"DON'T DO THAT, BARRIE! YOU SCARED ME!"**

But that made Barrie start barking right in my face. I dropped the lead and kicked the little living-room table, which had a lamp on it.

There was a loud crash and Barrie was barking again. Suddenly, I saw the lamp, in pieces on the floor, and I felt embarrassed. I realized I was shouting, and angry, and then Mum came in.

"What," she said, **"is going on here?"**

Chapter Seven
Carrie

"**Don't worry, Mum,**" I said, picking up the lead. Laurence had run out of the living room, so I guided Barrie into the hallway. "**It's fine. All good.**"

I find it helpful to think of Barrie as if he's a massive ship. You wouldn't run on to a massive ship and turn the key to start the engines and immediately screech off across the water, would you? No! You have to pull up the anchor and untie the ropes that are keeping it tethered to the dock. And then you start the engines, the massive humongous engines in the basement of the ship, and they slowly grind to life. Next, you have to check in all directions to make sure it is safe to depart, and then slowly, ever so slowly, you increase the power of the engines and the giant ship will begin to move, safely and steadily away from the dock.

The ship is *big*, so things take *time*. It's the same with Barrie. He's not a little tiny yappy dog that can bounce across a room and zigzag this way and that as soon as he wakes up.

But I don't want to make him sound like he does *everything* in slow motion. Once he's up and running, he *can* zip around. You should see him in the park chasing a frisbee or a ball. Barrie can move. Not always with perfect coordination, but he can move. However, on a cold evening just before Christmas, when it's dark outside and he's been asleep for an hour, it takes a while. You have to be patient.

That's something Laurence struggles with. He

doesn't have much patience. He's great at other things, though. Like his imagination... Sometimes I watch him in the garden as he fights invisible enemies for *hours*. It's like creatures and dragons and demons and warriors and wizards are coming at him from all angles, and he's bravely and skilfully defeating them. He sees them so clearly in his mind. I would feel self-conscious and silly because really there's nothing there. But, for Laurence, there *are* things coming at him. His imagination brings them to life, and he fights and makes sound effects and shouts and talks until Mum or Dad tell him to stop.

I opened the front door, with Barrie at my side. Laurence was already standing on the pavement in front of the house, a dark look on his face. He'd be all right in a minute. It was best not to mention what had just happened – the clouds in his mind would vanish and he'd find it easier to talk again.

If I get in a bad mood, it can stay with me for ages, days sometimes, but Laurence can go from joy to sadness and back to joy again in seconds.

It was cold outside and the street was quiet. A few houses on our street had Christmas decorations outside or in the window. Gavin Turtle's house, two doors down from ours, had the most decorations. Lights everywhere, a Santa hanging off the roof like he's climbing up, and a lit-up reindeer in the front garden.

Barrie waddled down the three steps from our front door and we walked out of the little gate at the end of our small garden. All three of us knew we'd turn left and walk round the block in that direction. We've always done it that way – I don't know why.

Barrie came to life. He shook his whole body, trotted over to the bush outside Mrs Daniels' house next door and gave it a sniff. Then he crossed to

the other side of the pavement and cocked his leg, peeing a bit over the front tyre of her car.

He's such a big dog that it's really always him walking me rather than the other way round. When he surges forward to look at or smell something, there's not much I can do about it. Walking Barrie is lots of getting yanked this way and that. He will respond if you tell him to stop or heel or sit – he's well trained – but if he's determined to go in a particular direction, you can't stop him. So we headed down the pavement and I lurched and stumbled after him, with Barrie's big tail bouncing in front of me.

Laurence was silent, so I said nothing. He'd speak when he was ready.

It was as we reached the red postbox on the street corner that it all went bananas.

Chapter Eight — Barrie

It started as a walk like any other walk. I had a quick pee against the first car as usual, had a bit of a body shake. I was getting *into* it.

So I was leading Carrie and Laurence down the pavement and it was all looking pretty normal. Couldn't see any other of my dog mates, but that's not unusual for an evening walk. In the morning, I'd expect to see them all.

Rocky Hamilton, the Scottish terrier who lives across the road – he's a good guy. Terrible breath, though. Everyone too polite to say anything but phew-ee. His breath could stop clocks.

Then there's Daphne Harcourt, the giant poodle who lives next door to Rocky. She has a ridiculously high opinion of herself. If she had two heads, she'd kiss herself.

Old Thunder Patterson, the mongrel who lives in the corner house – he has problems with his memory and you sometimes see him wandering around with a lost look on his face. Sad, really.

THUNDER PATTERSON

· DUSTY COOPER ·

And round the corner is Dusty Cooper. She's originally from Portugal and speaks in an accent so strong I can't understand a word she says.

I see those four almost every day.

Then you can bump into all sorts in the park: Lilly B the greyhound, Garbanzo the corgi, Teddy the Staffy, Truman the pug – you never know who you'll come across. Lots are friendly. Most I'm glad to see; a couple I pretend I haven't noticed in case they trap me into a conversation that might go on for hours. Dougald the cockapoo's the worst. Man, that dog is boring! All he talks about is his wretched fur and how he needs a trim or has just had a trim or is thinking about getting a trim or how it's more curly than usual or how it's less curly than usual or how he can't see properly because his face fur is too long or how he wants to get a fade like his owner and on and on and on. **"Who cares, Dougald?"** I want to yell at him. **"I'll tell you who cares! NO ONE!"** But I don't. I just sniff his bum politely and pretend I'm listening and try to work out how to get away. Seriously dull.

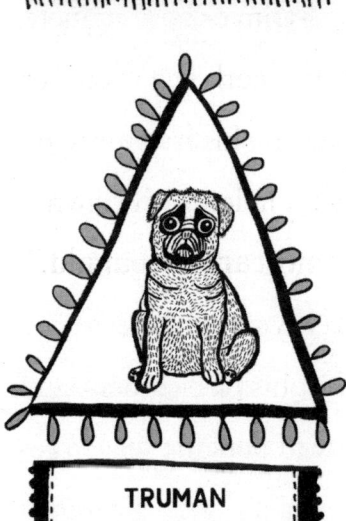

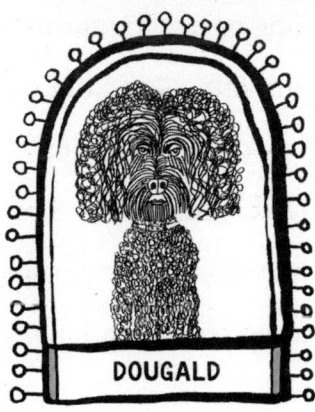

So it was a classic cold winter evening. Not too windy. Dry. All as per usual when I spotted Dorothea sitting on the front wall of the corner house, looking suspicious.

I can't tell you exactly why I thought she was looking suspicious because, let's face it, squirrels look fairly suspicious at the best of times. But she was acting strangely. She was up to something – I just knew it.

It was unusual to see a squirrel out and about after dark, for starters. Also, when she was near ground level, she'd normally be on the move. Squirrels don't tend to hang about on street corners, chilling. That's not their thing. They are always busy, busy, busy. But on that evening she was sitting on the wall, looking intently round the corner, away from us, staring at something I couldn't see.

Without thinking, I slowed my pace. Dorothea

didn't seem to notice us. She just sat there, peering down Fitzrave Road.

Was this my chance to catch her? My chance to teach her a bit of respect for me? To show her that I may be old but I'm not washed up?

I didn't want to *hurt* her – I'm not a monster. Maybe place a paw on her tail to stop her from getting away while I explained to her that my garden is my garden, and if she wants to walk through it, then she needs to ask permission. That she needs to stop grabbing the juiciest flowers from our bushes and eating them in front of me like I'm not there. It's not polite behaviour. Squirrels, like everyone else, should be polite and respectful and considerate. That's all I wanted to say.

Closer and closer we got to her and still she didn't stir. This was bizarre… This was not normal – but this was my chance.

Casually I glanced round to see who was holding the lead. Carrie. This was good. She held the lead lightly, and I knew that if I leapt forward, it would fly right out of her hand. Laurence, on the other hand, often wrapped the lead round and round his wrist, which meant that if I suddenly sprinted after Dorothea I'd drag him with me. I didn't want to hurt one of the kids.

Laurence looked at me as I turned my head in his direction. I raised my eyebrows as casually as I could, as if to say, *Hey. Nice evening. All normal. Nothing to see here. Carry on*, but who knows if he understood that.

Focusing ahead again, I was surprised that Dorothea *still* hadn't noticed us coming.

A few more steps, I thought. *Please don't turn round, please don't turn round, please don't turn round. A few more steps and it's go time…*

Dorothea didn't turn. And I seized my chance.

I surged powerfully forward, the lead flying out of Carrie's hand as predicted. In two mighty bounds I took off, my magnificent frame rising high into the night air, my eyes focused on the target, my body fizzing with excitement.

Chapter Nine — Carrie

Everything was fine – even though Laurence still wasn't speaking – until just before we turned left on to Fitzrave Road, at the corner where the postbox is. Barrie suddenly ran forward, yanking the lead from my hand, and he jumped face first into the wall of the Pattersons' front garden. I don't know what he was trying to do, but that must have hurt.

He fell sideways on to the pavement, rolled over, then got up and charged away down Fitzrave Road, the lead bouncing behind him.

"**Barrie!**" I shouted, running after him. "**BARRIE!**"

Chapter Ten

Laurence

We were walking along, me trying not to stand on the cracks in the pavement, when Barrie jumped face first into a wall before zooming off, with Carrie chasing after him.

I stopped. I wasn't running anywhere. Whatever weird game they were playing, I wanted no part of it.

I was standing right in front of the postbox. I looked at it. I must have passed this postbox a million times – it was on the way to school; it was on the route round the block when we took Barrie for a walk; it was on the way to the shops; it was on the way to the tube; it was on the way to the park. I passed it again and again and again and again, and it occurred to me that I had never looked at it properly before. I guess I was usually thinking about something else.

I noticed that Barrie, halfway down Fitzrave Road, had stopped at the gates of the big house on the left and was barking furiously at something on the other side of them. I could hear Carrie trying to soothe him.

I turned back to the postbox – just as the little door in the front swung open, revealing a short creature with large eyes, a neat beard and a floppy hat, standing on a pile of letters.

When I say short, I mean *short*. Probably about the height of a three-year-old, but this bloke had a beard so who knows what age he was. He was how I'd always imagined a goblin might look, or an elf or even a leprechaun: rosy cheeks, pointy chin, big messy eyebrows.

He looked at me. I looked at him.

I said nothing. I had never met a goblin – or an elf or a leprechaun – in a postbox before. Life doesn't prepare you for moments like this.

Before I could think of something to say, he reached out, grabbed the door and closed it.

What was I supposed to do now?

I tried to open the door. I had questions. I wanted to know why he was standing inside a postbox and how had he got in there and was he always in there? Did the Post Office know about him? What did he do in the dark all day? Read our letters? Had he seen the letter to my granny I'd posted a few weeks ago? So many questions.

The door was locked. I peeked in through the letter slot but couldn't see anything. I put my mouth to the slot.

"**Hello,**" I said.

Nothing.

I tried again, louder.

"**Hello?**"

Nothing.

"**The thing is,**" I continued, "**I know you're in there because I just saw you. My name is Laurence. I live up the road. I walk past this postbox every day. I have a dog called Barrie and sometimes he pees on it, so I'm very sorry if you were in there when he did that. He's a good dog. Can I talk to you for a moment? Hello?"

"Laurence?"

I looked round to find Carrie, holding Barrie by his lead, watching me talk through the slot of the postbox.

"Laurence," she said, "what are you doing?"

Chapter Eleven
Barrie

Jumping on to a wall at high speed is not an easy thing to do, and I have to admit that this time I had got my calculations wrong. You have to factor in wall height, distance, angle of approach, wind direction, take-off point, landing point and much more.

It had started well. I was in mid-air before that wretched squirrel, Dorothea, had any idea I was coming. I move well for a big dog. For a big *old* dog, I'm nimble.

But I had forgotten one important thing and it proved crucial. As I burst forward, I guessed that the lead would fly out of Carrie's hand with no resistance. I was half right. It flew out of her hand, yes, but she had been holding on quite tightly and this meant there was a slight pull on the lead before it popped free. This, in turn, meant my run-up speed was slower than expected, with the result that, instead of flying through the air and landing delicately on Dorothea's tail, I jumped head first straight into the brick wall.

And it hurt.

Dorothea was alerted to my presence and took off down the road. I quickly jumped to my feet and followed her at speed. I would have caught her too if she hadn't slipped through the big gates of the house where that snooty cat Moley lives. Dorothea took the coward's way out.

I stopped at the gates and tried to explain to Dorothea that I meant her no harm but that

I had a few thoughts on respect and manners that I wanted to talk to her about. However, Carrie arrived soon after and shushed me.

I could see Dorothea hiding up a small tree in the front garden, watching me with those sharp little eyes, and I gave her a look to say, *This isn't over,* but I have no idea if she was bright enough to get the message.

Dorothea smirked at me. At least I think it was a smirk — you can never tell with squirrels.

Behind her, Moley was in the upstairs window, checking to see what the fuss was.

Squirrels are basically thieves: they steal nuts and flowers and other foods, and they bury them, then forget where most of their buried stashes are. It's an odd life, a selfish life – one of absolutely no benefit to the wider community. Can you imagine a squirrel risking their life in dangerous weather to save someone like we St Bernards do? No, me neither.

So I decided to be calm and dignified, to lead by example, to show this grotty little squirrel how a classy animal behaves. I stood quietly while Carrie picked up my lead. I listened patiently while she (I assume) told me off for running away like that. And, as we walked back towards Laurence standing by the red thing, I – calmly and with great dignity – stopped to do a poo on the pavement.

Chapter Twelve

Carrie

It's not like Barrie to run off like that. I don't know what spooked him. He didn't go far, though. I grabbed his lead, waited while he did his business, picked it all up in a poo bag and joined Laurence back at the postbox.

Laurence had his mouth to the slot for letters and was shouting into it. If anyone else did that, I'd wonder if they were OK but, as I said before, Laurence loves playing games. He has an amazing imagination. Still, this was a *bit* weird, even for Laurence.

"Laurence?" I said, to get his attention.

He turned his head to look at me.

"Laurence, what are you doing?" I asked.

When he didn't answer, I said, **"We need to go. The shop will be shutting soon. It probably shuts early this close to Christmas."**

"He's in there!" Laurence burst out. **"He's tiny and he's in there! I saw him!"**

"Who's in there, Laurence?"

"I don't know who he is."

"Then open the door and let him out," I said. It was always good to play along with Laurence's games. He got cross if you said, *What spaceship?* or *There are no elephants in here*, or whatever. His imagination was so good it was as if he really saw the things he was imagining.

But it was cold and we had to get to the shop and I didn't want this to turn into a whole big thing.

"The door's locked," he said. "He locked it from the inside."

He put his mouth to the letter slot again.

"**PLEASE!**" he shouted into it. "**OPEN UP!**"

He put his ear to the slot, and we stood and listened. Nothing.

"**We should go...**" I said.

"**It's just rude!**" said Laurence, and he reached out, grabbed the warm poo bag from my hands and shoved it through the slot and into the postbox!

My mouth dropped open.

"**Laurence! You can't put a full poo bag into a postbox! That's disgusting!**"

"**Then he should have answered me!**"

"**Disgusting!**" I repeated. "**Absolutely revolting!**"

Then I turned and marched off with Barrie in the direction of the shops.

Chapter Thirteen

Laurence

I knew I shouldn't have put the poo bag in the postbox. I just lost my temper. I hate it when people ignore me.

I trudged after Carrie and Barrie to the shops. I was cross with myself and cross with them and cross with the goblin or elf or whatever it was. A black cloud filled my head. I hate not being understood. I hate being confused.

I wasn't going to catch up with my sister and Barrie at the speed I was going, but that was fine by me. I didn't want to speak to anyone. I saw Carrie look over her shoulder to check whether

I was following them. She tried to disguise it by pretending she was giving Barrie a scratch, but I could see her glance in my direction. She was probably worried that I'd stomped off somewhere. Let her worry. She should have believed me about the tiny man.

She waited for me outside the little supermarket. She passed me Barrie's lead and, without a word, walked into the shop, coming out a couple of minutes later with the mince pies. I heard Christmas music coming from inside the shop as she opened the door. We headed home again. No one said anything. Carrie and I could both be stubborn like that, not wanting to be the one to speak first after a fight. It was like if you spoke first, you lost.

I normally won because I could go for days without saying anything. Once, after an argument over who had killed the Tamagotchi that Carrie had got for Christmas and that we'd agreed to look after together, I didn't speak to her for four days. Four whole days! It eventually made her so upset she started crying. She told me I was the worst brother in the history of the world and that just because she was mostly positive about life it didn't mean she couldn't be hurt, and I felt so bad about making her upset that, even though I won, I felt like I'd lost.

But this time was different. I wanted to lose. I was going to speak first. I—

"Carrie, look!"

I couldn't help it. The words tumbled out. And Carrie didn't gloat or say she'd won. Because the reason why I spoke was that – as we turned the corner and crossed the road – we saw the poo bag being pushed out of the postbox before dropping with a plop on to the ground.

Chapter Fourteen

Barrie

I thought we were going to go straight home from the shops, which would have suited me because it was pretty chilly out, but Carrie and Laurence stopped next to the red thing on the corner *again* and started arguing *again*.

The red thing normally smells of Daphne Harcourt, the giant poodle who lives across the road. She claims she only pees on it because it's owned by the king and that she never pees on lamp posts or trees because they are common. I know that's not completely true because I've seen her peeing on the big tree at the entrance to the park twice. Daphne is very stuck-up. She calls herself a **"giant poodle"** when there's no such thing. Her breed is **"standard poodle"**, but she doesn't want to think of herself as **"standard"**. Her owners get her groomed loads too, which makes her even more big-headed. You see her trotting along with her nose in the air like she owns the place.

Anyway, the red thing is where Daphne pees most often and you can normally get a strong whiff of her whenever you pass it – but today there was another smell mixed in with hers. An unusual smell. One I'd never come across before. It's difficult to describe smells in words, but it was a musty, damp smell, like wet clothes mixed with wood smoke and some animal that I couldn't quite place. Possibly a dog. It was like a dog smell but not any dog I'd ever met. Definitely not from any dog around here because I know all those smells really well. Dog smells are usually warm, or rather they remind you of warm (I told you smells are hard to describe), but this one felt ice-cold. I don't know if I'm the only one who does this, but I divide smells into warm and cold. Mint is cold, but honey is warm, for example. This smell was about as cold a smell as you could get. Weird.

Laurence and Carrie were whispering fiercely at each other. I glanced around for Dorothea. Wretched squirrel was nowhere to be seen. She was probably too scared to come out after I flew through the air towards her. She was only safe because I misjudged the jump.

Then Laurence yelled something and ran off towards the house, but Carrie didn't budge and, because she was holding my lead, neither did I. I looked up at her and she looked down at me. She knew she could trust me and that she was safe as long as I was with her. Because I am the children's protector, ready to spring into action at any moment to defend them: a lean, mean protecting machine.

Chapter Fifteen
Carrie

Barrie stood there, panting with his tongue hanging out, a gooey string of dribble falling out of the side of his mouth, his big, watery eyes staring up at me. We'd only walked to the shop and back and you could tell he was already exhausted and looking forward to falling asleep by the fire. There was something about the way he held his head low that always made it look as if he was desperate to lie down.

I heard our front door slam in the distance. Laurence was angry with me again. I had admitted it was weird that the poo bag had fallen out of the postbox – but I'd said there had to be a rational explanation. I reckoned Laurence hadn't pushed it all the way in and gravity had slowly worked its magic until it eventually fell just as we saw it.

Laurence seriously expected me to believe he'd seen a real elf or pixie or goblin or something just standing inside the postbox! It was bonkers, even for him. He stormed off saying he was going to fetch some of Dad's tools and I knew there'd be no stopping him. I'd have to stay here and keep a lookout while he tried to open the little door with the tools, because I bet you can get in trouble for doing that and I'd never forgive myself if he got caught.

Also, once he opened it, we could prove there was no elf or whatever inside.

Soon, Laurence was sprinting back towards me, six or seven of Dad's tools in his hands. He said nothing as he threw them to the ground, knelt in

front of the postbox and tried to work out which tool would get the door open, the tip of his tongue poking out of his mouth.

So fierce was his focus and concentration when he was in this sort of mood that an earthquake could be going on around him and he wouldn't notice.

"**Laurence, what if aliens were real? What if they came from somewhere called Xarquon, and could go undercover as humans?**" I said, just to amuse myself as I knew he wouldn't be listening.

He said nothing, only put down one tool and tried another.

"**What if their true form on their home planet was a twelve-legged, two-headed creature with their brain in a plastic bag hanging from one of their necks?**"

Laurence put down that tool and tried another.

"**The plastic bag has their name written on**

it in Xarquonese," I continued. "One of the aliens is called Cameron. Cameron Long-Dribble. And he has four thousand, eight hundred and sixty-two brothers on Xarquon and they're all called Cameron too. It gets confusing."

There was a click and Laurence pulled open the door in triumph. I leant in to look.

Apart from a handful of letters, the postbox was empty.

Chapter Sixteen — Laurence

I couldn't believe it. Empty.

I had seen the tiny man with my own eyes. Staring right at me. As real as real can be.

And I had put the poo bag in through the letter slot. All the way in – I was a thousand per cent sure of that. And I had seen it pushed back out again as we came back from the shops. It had to be the tiny man who had done that.

But there was nothing inside the postbox apart from a few letters.

My mind danced with a million thoughts. Too many to cope with. So I knelt there, Dad's pliers in my hand, not knowing what to do next.

"Shall we shut the door and go home?" said Carrie. One of the good things about my sister was that she knew not to gloat about her being right and me being wrong. She knew that would annoy me.

I didn't reply. I was trying to think clearly. The tiny man must have been in there to push the poo bag out. And now he wasn't. So where had he gone? Carrie had been standing right by the postbox the whole time, so he couldn't have opened the door and sneaked off. So where else could he have gone? There had to be an explanation.

I put my hand inside the open postbox and felt the walls. Solid. No secret hiding places; no other way out. The goblin-elf had taken up almost all the space in there. He was simply too big to be in the postbox and not visible.

I took out the posted letters.

"**You shouldn't touch those,**" said Carrie. She was probably right, but I had to know. I tapped the bottom of the postbox. Metal. Solid.

I dropped the letters. I turned round. Both Carrie and Barrie were staring at me. Barrie, especially, seemed to have a **"give it up, mate"** look on his face.

I sighed and grabbed the postbox door to close it and, perhaps because I'd shifted my position slightly, I suddenly noticed a faint ring of light around the floor of the postbox. Was that light from the street lamp reflecting on the metal – or was it light coming from below?

Excitedly, I grabbed Dad's screwdriver and poked the inside edge of the bottom of the postbox. There was a thin gap between the base and the side. With a bit of jiggling, I slid the screwdriver into it. I tried to lever up the bottom but couldn't get a good angle on it. Then I tried the edge closer to the door. I pushed the screwdriver down and nothing happened. At first.

All of a sudden the base of the postbox tilted up. I got my fingers underneath it and lifted it clean out. It was solid metal and heavy and took a lot of effort, but out it came.

I dropped it on to the pavement where it fell with a clang. Carrie gasped.

I stuck my head into the postbox and peered downwards. Removing the base had revealed a hole – and below it was a passage.

I didn't hesitate. I came out of the postbox, then swung my legs into the hole and wriggled in. It was a tight squeeze, but I lowered myself down as far as I could, then dropped down into the hole. It was deep enough for me to stand fully upright under the postbox.

I glanced up at Carrie, who was watching me from above, a look of shock on her face.

"Come on," I said. "What are you waiting for?"

Chapter Seventeen
Barrie

The ice-cold smell got stronger as Laurence disappeared into the red thing. I barged past Carrie and stuck my head inside. Laurence was down below. My protective instincts took over and, without thinking about my own safety, I went in after him.

The trouble was that the hole was not quite big enough for me to fit in it and I got wedged halfway through. Which was embarrassing. I squirmed and I wiggled and sucked my tummy in and slowly slid further down until suddenly I was clear. I didn't so much jump as fall. I landed with a yelp on Laurence, who yelped too.

I then remembered that Carrie had been holding me on a lead and, before she could let go, she was almost yanked down through the hole too. She shouted something as Laurence and I stood up.

While she and Laurence talked through the hole, I looked around. It was dark down here,

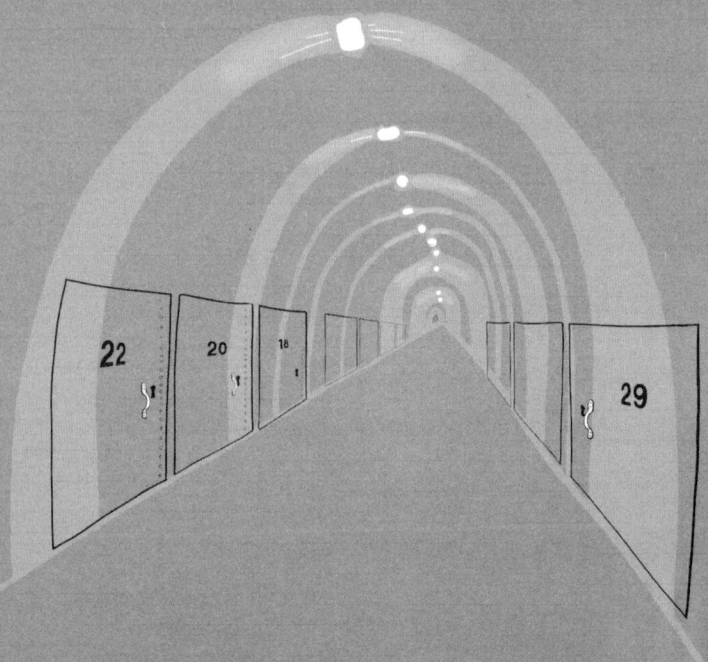

but there were dim lights in the ceiling. We were standing in a long tunnel that stretched off into the distance in both directions as far as I could see. Every so often there were little metal doors in the wall on both sides, with numbers painted on them. The ice-cold smell was even stronger, but there was now also a much more familiar smell coming powerfully from one direction. I started to walk towards it, but Laurence shouted my name, so I stopped.

He and Carrie were having a tense exchange, which ended with Laurence grabbing my lead. He started to walk down the tunnel, but we only went a couple of steps before he stopped. I sensed he was waiting for Carrie. Laurence relied more on me and his sister than he'd ever admit and I knew that, even though they argued a lot, he always felt happier when he was with her.

Carrie had swung her feet down into the hole and I could see she was trying to shut the door behind her. I heard a dog bark and knew instantly that it was Old Thunder Patterson. I would have barked too if I had seen someone climbing into the red thing.

Old Thunder probably wouldn't remember he'd even seen what he'd seen in a few minutes' time. *Would that matter?* I wondered. What if we ran into serious trouble down here and needed rescuing?

I thought about barking to let him know we were here, that he should spread the word to the others, but Laurence knelt down beside me, as if to say, *Keep quiet.*

I was impatient to explore, but I tried to remain calm.

Carrie dropped down into the tunnel; I could see she had shut the door of the red thing. She and

Laurence were looking around, trying to decide what to do – but I knew I had to take the lead here. There was only one direction in which we should be walking, and that was towards that familiar smell. That hateful, irritating, annoying, familiar smell.

Chapter Eighteen — Carrie

What were we doing? We shouldn't have been down there. I knew that much.

But there was no stopping Laurence when he had his mind set on something.

I wasn't sure which direction we should go, but Barrie set off at pace down the tunnel and we went with him. Might as well. We didn't have a better plan.

There were little doors in the wall at intervals, with numbers on them, and it didn't take long for me to realize they corresponded to house numbers on our street. All odd numbers on one side and even on the other. Our house was number 17 and, when we reached it, I tried to open the little door, but it was locked.

I said nothing to Laurence. He and Barrie were leading the way, and all three of us stayed silent. It was quiet down there. I had no idea what might be lurking.

Barrie seemed to know exactly what he was doing, though, and all Laurence could do was keep a grip on the lead as Barrie surged forward. Laurence glanced back at me, probably to make sure I was still there, his face a mixture of terror and excitement. I felt the same. This could turn out to be the most exciting day of our lives.

Or the worst.

We had been walking for probably a couple of minutes when we came to a junction. The tunnel continued straight on, but there was another one branching off to the right. I reckoned this was Edith Street, the road round the corner from our house where my lovely friend Grace lived.

Barrie didn't hesitate, turning right into the second tunnel and pulling Laurence behind him. The ceiling was lower in this tunnel, and Laurence and I had to crouch to avoid hitting our heads.

For the first time we heard noises, muffled to begin with but getting louder. Not noises I recognized. It sounded like hundreds of small dogs barking. I couldn't describe it any better than that. High-pitched yelping. Barrie started to run, and Laurence and I, still bent over, ran too. We passed number 36 – which I guessed was 36 Edith Street, Grace's house – but we didn't pause.

Suddenly Barrie stopped outside a door with no number on it. The sound of the little barking dogs – or whatever was making that noise – was coming from behind that door. Barrie looked to Laurence. Laurence looked to me. What were we going to do?

Before I could say anything, Laurence grabbed the handle and opened the door.

Inside was a chamber about the size of my bedroom but with a ceiling even lower than the one in the tunnel. The sound of barking dogs stopped and I realized that it wasn't dogs making the noise. It was squirrels, hundreds and hundreds of squirrels, now completely silent as they turned to the three of us standing in the chamber's doorway.

For a split second there was breathless quiet. They stared at us and we stared at them. What would you even say to a room full of squirrels?

"Hey, guys, what's up?"

"Good to meet you, squirrels. I'm Carrie, and this is my brother, Laurence, and my dog, Barrie?"

"Shoo?"

I figured the best thing to do might be to quietly close the door and go home and pretend this had never happened.

That many squirrels in one place were, to say the least, spooky. You only ever see one or two squirrels out and about together at most. Usually they're alone. Approximately three hundred squirrels packed into a small space, all staring at you in total silence … it made the hairs stand up on the back of my neck.

Then one of the squirrels moved. It turned to the wall and pressed a red button that I hadn't noticed before.

Instantly a shutter slammed down between us and the squirrels, red lights began to flash, and a siren started to howl.

We turned and ran. For a moment I forgot about

the low ceiling and scraped my head on the rough surface. It hurt.

I bent lower and moved as quickly as I could. I was ahead of the others, until Barrie came barging past me, lead flapping behind him. At the junction we turned left, retracing our steps. There were red lights flashing all along this tunnel too and the siren continued to blare. We reached the hole we had dropped through and stopped. A terrible truth occurred to me: the hole was too high for us to reach. We were trapped.

Laurence tried jumping to grab the edges of it, but he wasn't even close. He knelt down on all fours.

"**Stand on my back,**" he shouted above the din of the alarm. "**Stand on my back and try to climb up.**"

I did so and managed to grip the rim of the hole, but it was too difficult for me to pull myself up.

I tried a couple of times, but I wasn't strong enough. Maybe Laurence would have a better chance? I was about to step down and suggest it when the lights stopped flashing and the alarm fell silent. There were footsteps behind me and I swivelled round to have a look, carefully as I was still standing on Laurence's back.

"Good evening," the approaching voice said, still too far away for me to see the person properly. **"I hope I can be of some assistance. We shall need to look at that head of yours, young lady."**

I put a hand to my head. It felt wet. I checked my palm – blood. I glanced up again … as what could only be described as an elf walked into view.

Chapter Nineteen
Laurence

Carrie had quite a bad cut on her head, but the elf seemed to know what to do with it. (He was definitely an elf and not a goblin or a leprechaun.)

As he cleaned it up, I looked around his office. At least, he said it was his office, but it looked more like a store cupboard. There was one small chair, a wooden desk with a first-aid kit in the drawer, and a poster on the wall with writing that I couldn't understand.

I was a bit confused. The elf had looked really grumpy when I'd seen him standing in the postbox before, but meeting him down here he was all smiles and pleasant chat.

Mind you, I would probably have been grumpy if someone discovered my secret hiding place, so I couldn't blame him. And I couldn't blame him for pushing the poo bag out of the postbox. I wouldn't want to be wedged into that tiny space with a poo bag either. And he was being really kind to Carrie, chatting away as he sorted out her cut.

I looked to Barrie, who was lying down calmly, head on his paws.

If Barrie doesn't sense any danger, I thought, *then maybe there isn't any.*

I tuned back in to what the elf was saying.

"Yes, you certainly have discovered something top secret, you two."

At that moment, Barrie coughed, probably because it was quite dusty down here, but the elf glanced at him and nodded.

"Sorry, yes," he corrected himself. **"You three. Apologies."**

He looked nervously at Barrie, who, to be fair, was way bigger than the elf and must have seemed intimidating. The elf was not even half my height and was shorter than Barrie. When we'd first arrived in his office, which was a tight fit, Barrie had accidentally dribbled on to his head. The elf had tried his best to laugh it off, but I was sure it had unsettled him. I was going to tell the elf not to worry about the dog, that he was really a big softie, but the elf started speaking again before I had the chance.

"As I was saying, this is top, top, top secret and no one can know about it, so I have to ask you not to mention it to anybody."

Carrie winced as the elf dabbed her cut with antiseptic.

"Sorry, young lady," he said. "If I don't clean it up, it'll get infected."

"That's OK," said Carrie. "Can I ask you something?"

"Oh..." The elf sounded worried. "What?"

"What's your name?"

"Oh!" He looked relieved. "That's an easy one! My name is Spruce Motel. Pleased to meet you. And you are...?"

"I'm Laurence," I said. "That's my sister, Carrie, and our dog is called Barrie with an 'I-E'."

"'Barry with an I-E' is an unusual name."

"No, sorry," I said. "His name is Barrie, but

it's spelled with an 'I' and an 'E' instead of a 'Y' because of the guy who wrote *Peter Pan*."

"What's Peter Pan?"

"He's a boy who can fly and never grows up."

"Does he go to school with you?"

"No, he's in a book."

"He lives in a book?"

"No, he's a character in a book."

"Oh," said Spruce. "I don't like books."

Which was a strange thing to say because I get that a person might not like *some* books and I even get that a person might not like *most* books, but you can't dislike *all* books because some are amazing. You just have to find them. I'm always starting to read books and finding that I don't love them, but then you find a book that you do love and it's like the clouds have parted and golden sunshine pours from the sky and bathes you in a wonderful, warm light. It's like discovering magic.

"**Anyway, pleased to meet you all,**" said Spruce as he got a plaster for Carrie's cut, which had now stopped bleeding. "**But, again, I must insist that you tell no one about what you have seen.**"

"**What's all this down here for?**" I asked.

"**Oh,**" said Spruce Motel, smoothing the plaster on to Carrie's forehead. "**Look, I can't really tell you, but you should know that it involves Father Christmas...**"

"It's how you deliver presents, isn't it?" said Carrie. "**The tunnel leads to all the houses. Father Christmas doesn't come down the chimney – he uses the tunnel and nips into each house through the doors.**"

I was amazed. My sister was very clever sometimes. None of this had occurred to me.

"**Maybe,**" said Spruce carefully. "**Maybe that's**

true. But because the alarm went off, Father Christmas will want an explanation. I'm going to have to ask the three of you to come with me to the North Pole so that we can explain to him what happened. Then everything will be fine."

"Can't you explain to him what happened?" I said. "Why do we all need to go?"

"Because you were the ones who set off the alarm."

"We didn't," I said. "It was a squirrel."

"Yes, true," said Spruce. "Technically that's true. But they set it off because you were trespassing. Snooping about."

"We were only snooping about because I saw you standing in a postbox with the door open," I retorted.

"Well, you can tell Father Christmas that if

you want and I'll take the blame," the elf said breezily. "I don't mind. Let's go."

"If you don't mind taking the blame, then why do we need to go?" I asked.

"Look," said the elf, clearly making an effort not to get angry. "The rules are that if the alarm is set off, then whoever set it off has to report to FC and—"

"The squirrel set it off!" Carrie exclaimed.

"YOU HAVE TO LISTEN!" screeched the elf, his anger boiling over at last. His face went red and his big eyes became big.

Barrie slowly rose from his position on the floor and, towering over Spruce, opened his huge mouth as wide as it would go. It looked for a second as if he was about to bite Spruce's head clean off.

"I'm sorry," said Spruce meekly, clearly terrified. "I'm sorry. You're right. Forget the rules. I'll get a stepladder and help you go home. I'm so sorry. Follow me."

Chapter Twenty

Barrie

The strange tiny person took us into his office to look at Carrie's head. It was warm in there and soon I began to feel sleepy, so I lay down and put my head on my paws. Don't get me wrong – I'm a guard dog *all the time,* even when I'm feeling a bit sleepy, so I was ready to spring into action whenever needed. I'm never off-duty. But, like I said, it was warm in the office. I thought I'd have a little nap.

I didn't fall asleep straight away, which isn't like me. I lay there for a while thinking about all those squirrels as the others talked. There were *hundreds* of squirrels in that room and I can't pretend that the sight hadn't disturbed me. One squirrel was bad enough, but to see so many in one place all staring at me…

Look, I could handle myself, even against hundreds of squirrels. They would be no match for me. But I had questions. What were they doing there, for starters? Were they, perhaps, discussing me? Had Dorothea called a squirrel council and all the squirrels from across town had got together to decide what they were going to do to me? Or was I being paranoid?

And even if I was … just because you might be paranoid to think hundreds of squirrels have gathered together to plan an attack on you doesn't mean that the reason why they gathered together *wasn't* to plan an attack on you. Know what I mean?

Maybe not. I didn't particularly know what I meant with those questions, but I *did* know that

I was tired *and* a bit freaked out. Those two things were fighting each other in my head.

And, on top of that, I had cramp in my back leg. I needed to stretch it out.

I clambered to my feet with what I hoped was plenty of dignity. The room was so small that my head was almost touching the little fella's face, but my leg already felt a bit better. Then the tiredness hit me again and I yawned a pretty spectacularly big yawn right into the elf's face, which I felt a bit bad about because I'd only just met him, but I didn't have much choice.

Anyway, after I yawned at him, he started saying stuff very fast. Straight after that, he led us out into the tunnel and fetched a ladder. We climbed up and out of the hole – with Carrie pulling me up and Laurence holding me from behind – into the cold night air.

Laurence picked up the metal disc – which was propped against the wall of Old Thunder Patterson's house – and put it back inside the red thing. Then he dropped all the letters on top of it. Without a word, he closed the door to the red thing and locked it using Dad's tools, then he and Carrie and I ran as fast as we've ever run in our lives back to our house.

Once we were inside, the two of them hugged me and each other tightly, as if they'd never hugged me before, and I noticed that they were both shaking, probably because they were cold. I think that was why.

Chapter Twenty-One
Carrie

I lay in bed, trying to make sense of what had happened. It all felt unreal, like a weird messed-up dream. I was still shaking, full of fear and excitement and shock.

Obviously neither Laurence nor I said anything to Mum or Dad. What *could* we have said? That we'd discovered an underground network of tunnels used by Father Christmas to deliver presents? That we'd stumbled into a room containing hundreds of squirrels? That an elf had wanted to take us to the North Pole to report to

Father Christmas after our trespassing had caused one of the squirrels to set off an alarm?

It was all so confusing. Part of me couldn't believe we hadn't taken the chance to meet Father Christmas. Has any child in history ever had that opportunity? Has anyone in history ever had that opportunity *and turned it down?* How would we have got there? How would we have got back? What would Father Christmas have said to us? Would he have been cross that we'd set off the alarm? Technically it had been a squirrel that had set it off, but you'd feel pretty daft standing in front of actual Father Christmas and saying, **"It wasn't me! Honest! It was a squirrel!"**

Would he be angry that we'd discovered his secret? Did this mean we wouldn't now be getting any Christmas presents?

Just when my mind was spinning with all these

questions, I suddenly remembered the room full of squirrels again. What were they doing there? Having a meeting? A party? Working? Were they prisoners? Part of some sort of squirrel religion? Forming an army? Or a choir? Or rehearsing a play? It felt as though anything was possible. You never saw two squirrels hanging out together normally. Three hundred in a room was so far from normal it made me start to shake again.

And then there was Spruce Motel, who had been kind to me, cleaning my cut and putting a plaster on it. But then really angry when we wouldn't go with him to see Father Christmas. Or FC as he'd called him at one point. Had we got the elf into trouble? Had we been selfish by not going? Would we get him sacked? Would Father Christmas refuse to deliver our Christmas presents?

And then from there my mind bounced over to the tunnels themselves and the little doors in the walls. What was behind those doors? If there was a way into our house from below, where was it? Our kitchen? Could Spruce Motel get into our kitchen? What about the squirrels?

In fact, I was sure I could hear them marching up the stairs! I listened hard and heard that yappy barking sound that the squirrels had been making *and* the pitter-patter of tiny squirrel feet. They were outside my door! I sat up in bed, my heart pounding and my breath rapid—

And I realized I had been half-dreaming. There were no squirrels. I had imagined it all.

I settled down and told myself to get a grip. I didn't want to be alone, though, so I took my duvet and pillow and went to Laurence's room. He was awake. He looked at me but didn't say anything as I lay down on the carpet by his bed and huddled tightly under my duvet. I don't remember too much after that. I think I fell into a deep, deep sleep.

Chapter Twenty-Two

Laurence

I woke up and got dressed into my school uniform and went downstairs to get some breakfast. Carrie was asleep on the floor next to my bed, but she must have been incredibly tired because she didn't wake up. I figured I'd let her sleep.

In the kitchen, Dad burst out laughing when he saw me.

"What's so funny?" I said, a bit irritated.

"Going to school?" he said. **"On Christmas Eve?"**

The penny dropped and I remembered it was the Christmas holidays and there was no school today

– I'd finished school over a week ago. I had slept really badly because my mind just wouldn't turn off thinking about everything that had happened and I still felt groggy. In my confusion, I had gone into autopilot and got dressed. I felt stupid and embarrassed.

"**Barrie's desperate to go out,**" Dad said. "**Which is not like him at all. He's been standing by the front door all morning. I'm going to take him for a quick walk. Why don't you come with me?**"

On a regular day, heading out into the cold first thing in the morning would be the last thing I'd volunteer for. I'd usually rather have a bowl of cereal and read my book, but, despite how weird last night had been, I was desperate to check out the postbox, to see if anything else about it looked strange in the daylight. Had I dreamt the whole thing?

"OK, sure," I said, trying to sound as casual as possible. "I'll get my coat."

Barrie looked up at me as I attached his lead on him. Half of me was glad he *couldn't* talk because I'd be worried about him giving the game away to Dad, and half of me wished he *could* talk because I would have loved to have taken Barrie aside and discussed all we'd seen the night before and find out what he'd made of it.

Leaving the house, I turned left towards the corner with the postbox, but Dad called out from the hall that he wanted to walk along the canal so we should go right.

I froze. I couldn't think of any excuse for going left.

"Come on, sleepy chops," said Dad, striding past me and walking up the road, away from the postbox. No excuse came to mind, so I followed.

As we headed away from the house, both Barrie and I couldn't resist turning to have a look at the postbox, but everything seemed normal. Then from across the road came a shout.

"Dusty! Stop!" It was old Mr Cooper, who was huge, and his dog, Dusty, who was not. Despite the difference in size, Dusty seemed to be dragging old Mr Cooper over the road towards us against his will.

"Sorry." Mr Cooper smiled, his big grey b e a r d

flapping in the morning breeze. **"Dusty seems to be on a mission this morning."**

Dusty made straight for Barrie, giving his bottom a good sniff. Not for the first time, I marvelled at this. Dogs were always sniffing one another's backsides and it mystified me. Why would you want to do that? Can you imagine if humans did the same thing?

"Good morning, Headmaster!" SNIFF, SNIFF.

"Good morning, Laurence!" SNIFF, SNIFF.

"Your bottom smells delightful this morning, Headmaster!" SNIFF, SNIFF.

"Why, thank you, Laurence." SNIFF, SNIFF. **"So does yours!"**

"Have you smelt the policeman's bum today?"

"No, I haven't. Any good?"

"Oh, marvellous."

It simply wouldn't happen, but dogs can't get enough of each other's bums. So Dad and I stood there while Barrie and Dusty had a good old smell, tails wagging furiously. Dad half smiled at Mr Cooper, and Mr Cooper half smiled back.

"**Nippy, isn't it?**" said Mr Cooper.

"**Isn't it?**" said Dad. "**Come on, Barrie. Have a good Christmas, Mr Cooper.**"

And off we walked, down the ramp to the canal.

I love the canal. It's like entering a whole different world. A world of water, birds, bridges and boats. We were right in the middle of the city, but it didn't feel like it down there. No cars, for starters. Just joggers and cyclists and dog walkers and prams. And water. One day I'd like to live on a canal boat. How amazing would that be, to live in a house that floats! If you got bored of where you lived, you could just untie the rope and head

away down the canal and find somewhere else. A different view every week.

Wood smoke was coming out of the chimneys of the boats parked in a long line along the tow-path. I love that smell. I'd love getting up each morning and lighting a fire, then sitting on my deck.

Today, though, all I could think about was Spruce Motel and those squirrels. The squirrels!

So many of them. I looked around but couldn't see any nearby. Maybe they were all underground now, crammed into that little room?

The old Australian bloke who lives on the corner, down the road from us, hobbled slowly into view. He has a prosthetic leg that he claims was bitten off by a crocodile, but Dad reckons he was born like that. He has a dog as well – Thunder – but poor Thunder's best days are behind him now, a bit like his owner, and he too shuffled towards us.

Barrie, towering over Thunder, gave the smaller dog's bum a good sniff and Thunder returned the favour. Dogs are so weird sometimes. They were having a good old smell this morning for some reason while Dad and Mr Patterson had a chat. Dad is so embarrassing when he talks to anyone with a foreign accent because he always starts doing the accent himself, and today was no different.

He started finishing his sentences with phrases like **"fair dinkum"** and **"you little ripper"** and then, when the dogs had had enough of a nose of each other's bottoms, he walked on, wishing Mr Patterson **"G'day"**. I don't think he even knows that he's doing it.

We walked under the bridge and round the corner where there's a floating restaurant that serves Japanese food. On the other side of the canal, a tiny dog, so tiny it looked like it should be battery operated, stood on the roof of a boat and yapped across the water at us. Barrie stopped and looked towards it before Dad gave him a small yank on the lead and we carried on.

Another dog approached Barrie: the poodle from over the road. Her owner was on one of those weird one-wheeled scooter-type things that you clamp between your ankles and whizz about on.

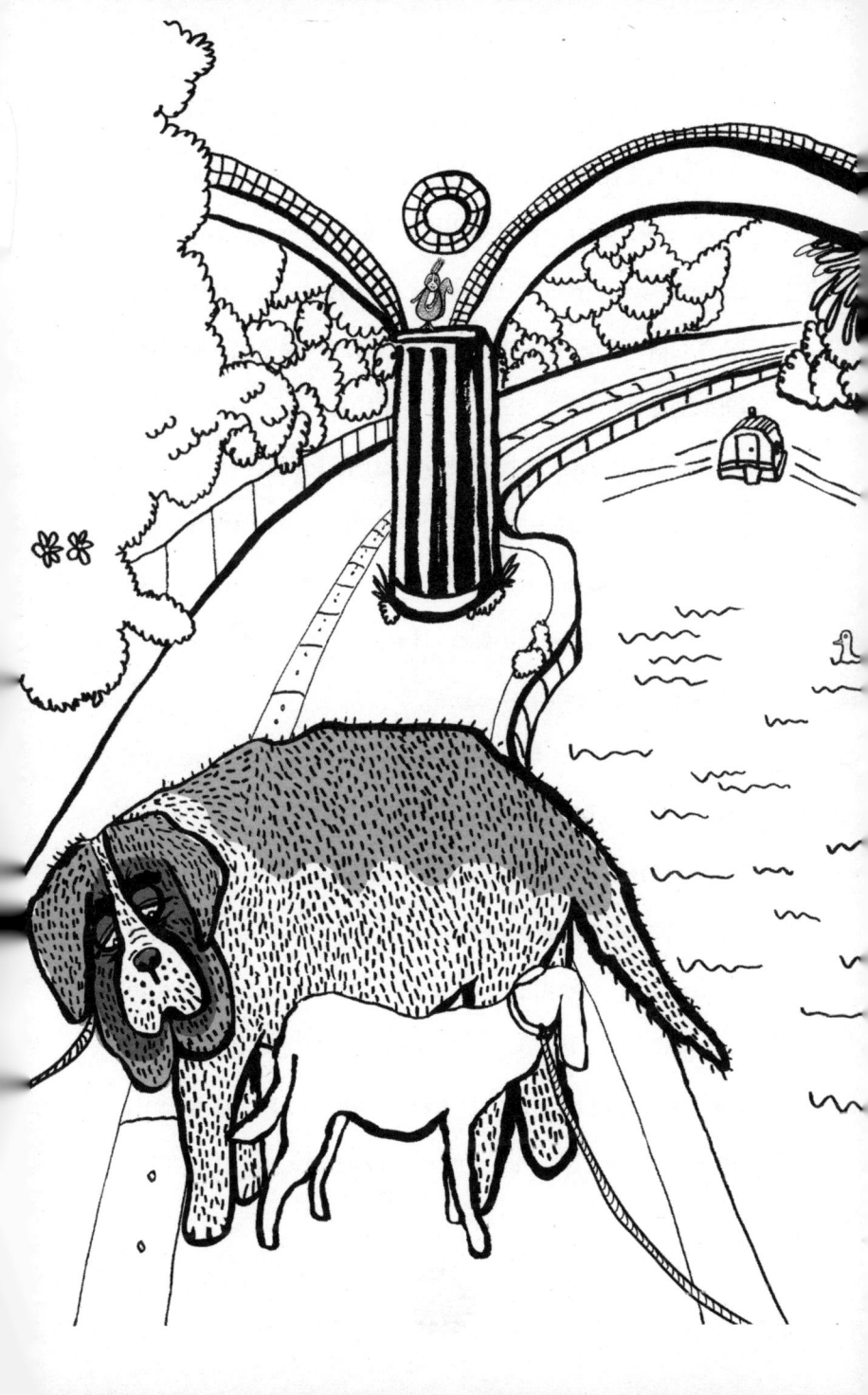

"**Daphne!**" shouted her owner (a young woman with a posh accent – I don't know her name) as she disappeared into the distance. "**Daphne, come on!**"

Daphne sniffed Barrie's bum, and Barrie sniffed Daphne's.

Daphne, what a strange name for a dog. People do call their dogs the strangest things. My friend at school has a dog called Nigel Havers – don't ask me why. Daphne trotted off after her owner and we carried on along the canal.

The dogs were coming thick and fast by this time – everyone seemed to be out. Rocky, the terrier from across the road, was next, but Barrie seemed less pleased to see him and tried to keep walking as Rocky barked and yipped and yelped excitedly in Barrie's face.

Up and out of the canal, into the park, we followed a well-worn route. A twenty-minute loop that we did all the time and that gave Barrie enough of a walk to stretch his legs and do his business but wasn't so long that everyone got tired out.

Barrie got taken off the lead once we entered the park. Usually he would have a gentle trot around or lope along next to us.

But not today.

As soon as Dad unclipped his lead, Barrie shot off towards the bushes, running like a dog on a mission.

"Barrie!" shouted Dad, alarmed. He turned to me. **"What's up with him?"**

I shrugged, acting innocent but feeling guilty. I couldn't help wondering if it had something to do with yesterday.

Chapter Twenty-Three
Barrie

All morning I'd been bursting to get out for my walk and not just because I was desperate for a pee.

I wanted to ask around about the tunnels we'd discovered last night. And I needed to warn everyone that the squirrels seemed to be organizing something. We dogs needed to be vigilant. I've never trusted those pesky squirrels and finding so many of them scheming together underground only increased my suspicions.

Annoyingly, though, the first dog I came across was Dusty, who is perfectly nice and everything, but she was desperately trying to tell me something and, frankly, I couldn't understand a single word because she was talking so fast. It sounded like she was saying something about bananas and carpet cleaners, but that couldn't be right. Frustrating. I didn't even get to tell her about the squirrels.

Next, we bumped into Old Thunder Patterson and he said he had an urgent message for me but the poor bloke couldn't remember it. Then he asked me if I knew the best way to eat cabbage, which can't have been the urgent message.

Then, further along the canal, Julian Tutt, the cute fluffy white Westie who lives on a houseboat, was yelling something at me across the water, but his voice is so high and yappy that I couldn't make out what he was saying. This was becoming infuriating. Clearly there was some big news out there, but Dusty, Thunder and Julian were all, for different reasons, the wrong dogs to get it to me.

Then, finally, Daphne bounced over and, as we gave each other's bums a good sniff, she told me the news: Dorothea was desperate to talk to me and she'd be waiting for me by the conker tree near the tennis courts in the big park. All the dogs who Daphne had met that morning had been talking about nothing else – it was the big news of the day. Apparently Dorothea had put the word out and said it was super urgent. Daphne spoke crisply and precisely, and didn't waste any time hanging around. Once she was happy I'd got the message, she trotted off after her owner.

However, that wasn't the end of it, because further on we passed Rocky, who I think I've already said has the worst breath in the known universe. It's so bad I'm surprised plants don't wilt and die as he walks past them. He came running over in a state of supreme excitement and was all in my face, telling me that Dorothea wanted to see me and I kept saying, **"I know!"** and backing away to avoid his rancid breath before it burnt my eyebrows off. His breath makes bin juice seem like perfume.

We got to the park, and I knew Dad would unclip the lead and that would be my chance to find Dorothea. I was aware that running off would worry Dad and Laurence, but what could I do? There was no way round it.

The lead came off and I went for it. I could hear Dad and Laurence shouting after me, but I ignored them. Dorothea and I were enemies – if she wanted to speak to me, something very important must have been happening.

I deliberately set off in a different direction to the conker tree. I didn't want Dad and Laurence to find me too quickly. Then, once I was in the trees and out of sight, I took a right turn along a fence, then doubled back and round to the conker tree. I could see Dad and Laurence running in the wrong direction. I reckon I had a few minutes before they found me.

At the tree there was no sign of Dorothea. I cursed her under my breath. Squirrels are so untrustworthy and flaky. I sometimes think there is nothing between their ears but air. I couldn't bark without alerting Dad and Laurence to my whereabouts, so I paced back and forth impatiently, muttering to myself. Dorothea was probably burying nuts, which, let's face it, is pretty much all squirrels do: find nuts, move nuts, bury nuts, forget where they buried the nuts, start all over again. It's a mindless life without much purpose or dignity. I'm glad I'm a dog with a proper job, protecting the two best children in the world.

After a few seconds, I heard Dorothea's voice from above and glanced up to see her on a low branch, eating, you'll never guess, nuts.

"You're out of shape, Barrie," she said to me.

"Am not!" I replied, annoyed.

"Look at you, panting like you've run miles. You only came from over there."

"Is this why you wanted to see me?" I said, trying to pretend I wasn't out of breath, which I was. **"To insult me?"**

"I have something important to tell you, but I'm worried all you can hear is your own wheezing."

"Just tell me. I don't have long." I looked around nervously. Dad and Laurence were some distance off but getting closer. I could hear them calling my name.

"You discovered our little operation last night," continued Dorothea, "and, while I'm not going to tell you all the details of what we do, it's important that you understand the basics so that you'll be able to help us."

"I'm listening."

"For some years we've been working with a man called Father Christmas – you may have heard of him. White beard, red clothes, lots of ho-ho-ho-ing."

"Of course I know Father Christmas," I said.

"I see him once a year."

"Right, well," Dorothea said, "the expanding world population meant his job was getting harder and harder every year. More and more children in the world, more and more presents to deliver each Christmas Eve. Eventually he had to make some changes. Father Christmas decided that the most important thing was

that children get presents on time and it was not so important that they were flown in that evening on his sleigh. So a couple of years ago he started pre-delivering presents to some houses, leaving them nearby, so they could be easily moved in on Christmas Eve. It worked. It saved him a huge amount of time."

"Right," I said, thinking, *But what has this got to do with me and Carrie and Laurence?* So I said that.

"But what has this got to do with me and Carrie and Laurence?"

"Patience," said Dorothea, taking a bite out of an acorn and then talking with her mouth full, which is just rude. Squirrels are so *fidgety*.

"Father Christmas's elves dug tunnels under the streets so that the presents can be safely left next to the house or flat they're going to be delivered to. The presents are put in the tunnels in November and then it's easy to deliver them all on Christmas Eve. Father Christmas doesn't even need to squeeze down any chimneys; there are routes into every house from these tunnels. Saves a lot of time, believe me. It's a great system and works brilliantly. He asked us squirrels to keep the tunnels in good order and check the presents are protected."

"Really?" I said, finding it hard to believe anyone would trust a squirrel with such an important job.

"Really," said Dorothea.

I could hear that Dad and Laurence were getting closer.

"Get to the point, Dorothea," I said. "I'll have to go any second."

"The issue," said Dorothea, suddenly sounding much more serious, "is that elf."

"Spruce Motel?"

"Spruce Motel, exactly. He isn't supposed to be down there at all. The elves are meant to stay and direct operations from the North Pole. That elf is up to no good."

"Maybe he's checking up on you squirrels?" I said. "I would."

"Presents have been going missing," said Dorothea, "including Laurence's new bike."

Now, this *was* serious. Laurence was desperate to get a bike. Not getting one would be awful. It would ruin his Christmas.

"And Spruce Motel has been doing all sorts of things he shouldn't, like appearing in public the other night when your boy saw him. That's a massive problem. No elf should ever be seen by a human. He's up to something and it's not good – and I bet FC doesn't know about it."

"Sounds bad," I said. "But what can I do about it?"

"I don't know, but there's nothing we squirrels can do. And now that your boy and your girl have seen the tunnels and met Spruce, I thought they might help. We don't know who else to turn to."

"Ah, I see. You squirrels can't handle it so you need us dogs to fix it for you."

"We need the humans to help us," said Dorothea. "You're just the messenger."

"You want me to climb up there and teach you a lesson?"

"You couldn't climb this tree to save your life."

"How dare you! You need to show me more respect!" I snapped.

"Wanna make me?"

"Oh, big talk for such a small animal!"

"You're too scared to help!" Dorothea sneered.

"Am not!"

"Am too!"

"OK," I yelled. "I'll help! Happy now? I promise I'll help!"

I realized that I was barking loudly then. I had lost my cool. That squirrel winds me up so much.

Dad and Laurence had obviously heard because they ran over and clamped the lead on me. Dorothea took off through the treetops and, after a ticking-off from Dad for running away, I turned and headed for home with him and Laurence.

I was worried all the way back. If that pesky squirrel was telling the truth, Christmas could be in danger, and I knew how upset Laurence and Carrie and all children would be about that. But what could I do?

Chapter Twenty-Four — Carrie

I woke up when Laurence and Dad got back. Laurence took me aside and told me that Barrie had been barking at a squirrel in the park. Normally I wouldn't have thought twice about it, but after what had happened down in the tunnels last night, we both wondered if something was going on.

Could squirrels and dogs communicate with each other? It seemed unlikely, but after talking to an elf and seeing a squirrel set off an alarm, well, anything now seemed possible.

"Should we tell anyone about what we saw last night?" I asked him.

"No," he said. "We promised Spruce that we wouldn't. And, also, who would believe us? I suppose we could show them the tunnels and the way into them through the postbox, but Spruce made it clear that would make things difficult for Father Christmas, which is the last thing we want."

So we got on with helping Mum and Dad with last-minute Christmas preparations and tried not to think about it. In our house, the Christmas tree doesn't go up until Christmas Eve, so we went with Dad to choose a tree, helped him carry it home and then unpacked all the decorations from boxes brought down from the attic.

My friend Sonya puts her tree up in November and can never understand why we wait so long to get ours. I don't really know why Mum insists on waiting that long, because then the tree and all the decorations get taken down on Twelfth Night (the sixth of January), so they're not even up for two weeks. Mum says it keeps Christmas special and that Sonya's family have theirs up for so long that they must get bored of it.

It drives me wild waiting till Christmas Eve to get the tree up, but I suppose it *is* incredibly exciting when the day finally comes, and Laurence and I love decorating it.

We have very different tree-decorating styles. I like to put every decoration I can find on the tree. **"The more, the merrier"** is my philosophy. But Laurence gets all arty about it and talks about themes and colour combinations. This year he only let me put white and red decorations on the tree. I didn't argue.

When Mum and I took Barrie out for an evening walk, though, I couldn't help but slow down at the postbox to check for any signs that the door had been opened. I even had a glance through the letter slot.

"What are you doing?" said Mum.

"Um. Looking for one of Father Christmas's elves," I said.

Mum burst out laughing. **"I don't think you'll find one in there,"** she said. She couldn't have known how wrong she was.

I noticed that Barrie seemed keener than usual to interact with other dogs, and every time we saw one, he'd strain at the lead to get to them. Barrie's so big that when he wants to do something it's hard to stop him. He even dragged us across the road a couple of times so that he could greet another dog. But all he did when he got to them was sniff their bums. He stopped to do it to every single dog being walked.

Mum was getting exhausted trying to control him and we laughed a lot while we were being dragged around the neighbourhood by our dog. Mum made the same joke to everyone we met to cover her embarrassment:

"I'm not taking Barrie for a walk – he's taking me! I should be the one wearing the collar!" she'd say.

Finally, even Barrie couldn't keep it up and he let us head home. As soon as we were in the door, he lay down in front of the fire and fell fast asleep, twitching as he dreamt of goodness knows what.

After dinner, we watched a movie together and Barrie slept right through that too. We always watch the same film every Christmas Eve, an old black-and-white film called *Miracle On 34th Street*, and it wouldn't seem like Christmas without it.

Then Laurence and I went to bed and, after lying there for a few minutes worrying about the elf and squirrels and Father Christmas, I fell asleep. So far, so normal. A Christmas Eve like any other.

So it was a shock to be woken in the middle of the night by Barrie biting the sleeve of my nightdress and literally dragging me out of my bed. I fell with a thump on to the floor.

"What are you doing?" I moaned, sleepy and confused, but Barrie had already left the room.

I lay there on the floor, wondering what was going on. Had Barrie completely lost the plot? He'd run away from Dad and Laurence, which wasn't like him. He'd dragged Mum all over the neighbourhood, which wasn't like him, and now he'd pulled me out of bed in the middle of the night, which *really* wasn't like him.

Perhaps, I thought, what had happened down the tunnels had disturbed him more than we had realized.

Then I heard a thump coming from Laurence's room and a sleepy Laurence saying, **"Barrie! What are you doing?"**

I went to his room. Laurence was lying on the floor, looking as confused as I felt. Barrie picked up Laurence's trousers and dropped them on Laurence's head, then ran out of the room.

"Has Barrie completely lost the plot?" asked Laurence, saying my question out loud as he pulled the trousers off his head.

Before I could answer, Barrie was back carrying my blue jumper in his mouth. He dropped it at my feet, picked Laurence's trousers up off the floor and dumped them on my brother's head again.

"I think," said Laurence, "Barrie might be trying to tell us something."

Chapter Twenty-Five
Laurence

I got dressed as quickly as possible. Then Carrie and I crept downstairs after Barrie. In the hall, Barrie picked up one of Dad's screwdrivers and offered it to me. It was clear what he was trying to tell us: we needed to open the postbox.

I grabbed what I needed. Carrie and I barely said a word to each other, but we didn't need to. We had both suspected that the story with the elf and the tunnels and the squirrels hadn't ended. We had both wondered what the next chapter in that story might be. I guess we were about to find out.

It also wasn't a surprise that Barrie was taking

the lead. He was more than a pet to us; he was like a big brother. A big hairy brother. A big hairy brother who had looked out for us our whole lives.

Once, on holiday in Cornwall, when I was two or three, I had wandered off down the beach without Mum and Dad noticing. They were busy changing a particularly interesting nappy that Carrie had filled, and were dealing with wipes and sand and trying to clean my sister. It was Barrie who spotted I'd gone. He'd dashed up and down the beach until he found me. I was happily playing in the shallow water of a rock pool, but he grabbed me by the collar, pulled me to my feet and shepherded me back to Mum and Dad.

I'd do anything for that dog, and I suspect he would do anything for Carrie and me.

So he wouldn't drag us out of bed in the middle of the night unless it was important. He must have

known something that we didn't. Well, I really hoped that was the case, because the trouble we'd be in otherwise didn't bear thinking about.

Once we'd wrapped up in several layers, Carrie opened the front door as quietly as possible and we stepped out into the winter night. It was *freezing*.

All three of us ran down the road to the postbox, partly because of the cold, partly because we were so tense and nervous. I got to work immediately and, within seconds, had the door open. I carefully removed the few letters that had been posted and handed them to Carrie so they wouldn't get damaged or lost, and turned my attention to the metal disc covering the base: the gateway to Father Christmas's tunnels. Carrie kept an eye out in case anyone saw us, but the streets were deserted. I wasn't even sure what time it was.

Almost immediately, though, I realized

something had changed. This disc had been locked from below. It wouldn't budge. Someone had bolted it in place.

"**This isn't going to open,**" I said to Carrie. "**Someone doesn't want us getting in this way again.**"

She looked crestfallen.

"**Any ideas?**" I asked.

She shook her head. Barrie shuffled past me and peered inside the postbox, his tail wagging furiously. From off in the distance we heard a shout – people out late on Christmas Eve – and I suddenly felt frightened. We shouldn't have been out there at that time of night. What were we thinking? How would we explain this to Mum and Dad if we got caught? "**Barrie told us to come out here and try to open the floor of the postbox**"? That sounded bananas.

I replaced the letters, closed the postbox door and locked it. Then Barrie, Carrie and I ran home. Once we were inside the front door and had closed it silently, we stood for a few moments shivering in the hallway, wondering what to do next.

Chapter Twenty-Six

Barrie

This was a disaster. If Laurence couldn't get us down into the tunnels, then how could I keep my promise to Dorothea? And a St Bernard never goes back on a promise.

When we got inside, though, Carrie said something to Laurence and then they both ran down the stairs to the cellar. I ran after them.

The cellar was somewhere I never went. It was spooky. It was a small narrow room under the house that smelt of damp and bricks. Dad used it to store things. It was messy down there: boxes piled up against the wall, two bikes and a roof box for the car, for when we went on holiday to the seaside.

Laurence closed the cellar door behind us and turned on the light, a single bare bulb hanging from the ceiling. The dim glow it gave off made everything feel weird.

He and Carrie started feeling along the walls with their hands. They were looking for something, but I didn't understand what.

I didn't know how to help, so I ran from Laurence to Carrie and then to Laurence again, seeing if they needed me. I wondered whether I should bark to show how excited I was, because I *was* excited and I really wanted to bark, but I decided against it. No one ever liked me barking at this time of night. That had been made very clear to me over the years, but sometimes you just can't keep it in.

I had so much energy that I didn't know what to do with it. I spun round and round on the spot a few times and then stood still, feeling slightly out of breath and dizzy.

Laurence was moving the bikes away from the wall on the other side of the cellar. Then he moved the boxes away from the wall too. He and Carrie were whispering to each other. It's frustrating being a dog sometimes – when you know something important is happening, but you don't know what it is. It feels like everyone else knows a secret, but won't, or rather can't, tell you what it is.

The temptation in a situation like this is to let the frustration and the excitement get to you and that's when the barking normally starts, but, again, I told myself I had to be strong. Barking would bring Mum and Dad downstairs, and I knew that wasn't going to help.

Laurence and Carrie were on their knees now, searching for whatever it was they were looking for on the floor. Feeling the tiles, which looked like they had been there for a thousand years. Well, a long time. They were rough and uneven. Laurence and Carrie were trying to lift tiles with their fingers without success. I wagged my tail even harder.

The urge to bark was almost overwhelming now. This was all so exciting and so confusing that I could hardly bear it. To stop myself from making noise, I went to inspect the area behind where the boxes had been and that's when I smelt it. Faintly at first, so faintly I assumed I had imagined it, but I took a deep breath and sniffed the wall again. No, I was right. That smell again. That unmistakable ice-cold smell.

It was coming from the other side of the wall. I ran my nose over different sections until I found the place where the smell was coming through the strongest. I lifted my paw and tried to push it open, but it was as solid as a … well … as solid as a wall. Because it was a wall.

I tried again and again – my paw on the cold hard brick, sniffing the scent, faint but lingering.

Then all at once Carrie and Laurence were beside me and they were also pushing against the wall. Could they smell it too? Or had they just seen what I was doing and were copying me?

I pawed at the wall again. So did Laurence. And Carrie. They stopped at last and then stood back, looking at the wall and frowning.

Carrie stepped forward and gripped the edges of one brick that was sticking out slightly, pulling it clean out towards us. It slid out with barely any effort. And in the gap it left was a tiny handle. Carrie pushed the handle down and a section of the wall opened away from us like a door. A door made of bricks. It revealed the tunnel we'd been in before.

We've done it! I thought. *Together!* We'd solved it together. I was so proud of us. I wanted to lick Carrie and Laurence's faces off.

But there I go again, getting carried away. We'd solved the problem of how to get back into the tunnels ... but I suspected there were further adventures awaiting us.

Chapter Twenty-Seven
Carrie

It was Laurence who climbed through the small opening first and into the dimly lit tunnel. I followed, and Barrie brought up the rear. It was totally quiet. There seemed to be no one about.

"**Where is everyone?**" I whispered to Laurence.

"**What do you mean?**"

"It's Christmas Eve," I said. "Shouldn't elves or squirrels or Father Christmas or someone be delivering presents right about now? They've got thousands and thousands of presents to deliver. Stuff should be happening."

"Maybe they've done it already and we missed it?"

"No, I checked under our tree when we got in. There were no presents from Father Christmas. And he hasn't touched the mince pie we left out for him."

"It probably all happens very quickly." Laurence shrugged. "I don't know."

He was trying to act relaxed, but I know my brother and I could tell he was frightened. His eyes darted up and down the tunnel. He, like me, was nervous.

But I trusted Barrie and I knew he must have had a good reason to drag us out of bed tonight. I bent down and scratched him on the top of his head in case he was nervous too.

"What is it, Barrie?" I said quietly. "Why did you bring us down here?"

Barrie licked my face with his big wet tongue.

"Why can't you talk?" I said to him, and then stood up again.

"Shall we go to Spruce Motel's office?" I said to Laurence. "We can ask him if everything is OK."

Laurence nodded and we headed off in that direction. As we walked, I tried a couple of the small doors that led to our neighbours' houses to see if they were open, but none of them were. Surely this tunnel should be full of wrapped presents if they hadn't been delivered yet? Wasn't this the biggest and busiest night of the year for these tunnels?

Spruce's tiny office was locked. We knocked on the door and waited for a moment. Laurence turned to me.

"I think maybe we should go home," I said. "We shouldn't be down here, and Barrie doesn't seem to have a clue what to do either."

We looked at our dog, who looked back up at us with his big, sad eyes.

Then Barrie's head snapped round and his ears pricked up. I listened hard, but my hearing wasn't a patch on his. I held my breath. Was this something good? Or the opposite?

Barrie took off down the tunnel; I'd never seen him run so fast. Then he skidded to a halt and glanced back at us, as if to say, *What are you waiting for?!*

Laurence and I, stunned by the sudden burst of energy from Barrie, recovered ourselves and ran after him. Once he saw we were following, Barrie took off again.

Barrie's a lot quicker than us, so he kept having to stop and wait for us. He barked at us twice, which I took to mean *Hurry up!* but a bit of me wondered whether it meant, *We're in terrible danger!*

We snaked through the tunnels, occasionally heading down dead ends and having to turn round and retrace our steps. There were loads of junctions and at every one Barrie would stop and listen hard before picking a direction and heading off again. All the tunnels looked the same, with rows of small numbered doors on either side, and they seemed to be completely empty except for us.

After we'd been running for a few minutes, I have to admit I was starting to wonder if Barrie knew what he was doing and wasn't leading us on a wild goose chase. The terrible thought crossed my mind that we were following a dog who might not have a clue what he was doing or where he was going. Was he just running for the sake of it?

Then I heard it.

A chant? Was that what it was? It was hard to tell. It was quiet and distant at first. It stopped, then started again. The sound of one word being repeated…

There again. Was the word … *chunks?*

The three of us ran towards it.

Barrie ran ahead, of course. Laurence was just behind – he's always been a faster runner than me. I was breathing hard by the time I caught up with them.

They had stopped and were standing outside a small closed door that was low down in the wall. It probably only came up to my knees – I wasn't sure I'd be able to get through it. It had a handle and a key in the lock.

There was the chant again, deep and loud: **"Chunks, chunks, chunks…"** Everyone spoke it at exactly the same time.

Barrie barked at us.

"**I think he wants us to open the door,**" said Laurence.

"**What do you think we should do?**" I replied.

Without waiting for an answer, Laurence knelt down and tried the handle. The door wouldn't open. He looked up at me, and then he turned the key.

Another chant of "**Chunks, chunks, chunks...**" It was scary but, again, we had to trust Barrie.

Laurence tried the handle once more. I was down beside him on my knees too.

The door opened and inside a thousand squirrels turned to stare at us and, as one, chanted, "**CHUNKS, CHUNKS, CHUNKS.**"

Chapter Twenty-Eight
Barrie

Have you ever been in a room with a thousand squirrels? Have you ever been in a *windowless* room with a thousand squirrels? Have you ever been in a windowless room with a thousand squirrels when the room isn't big enough to properly fit a thousand squirrels? I'm guessing **"no"** is the answer, so let me try to explain what a thousand squirrels smell like in those circumstances, because I want you to appreciate exactly how hard it was for me to walk into that room.

Take the smelliest pair of socks you can find, add the smelliest breath, stir in the smelliest cheese, add the smell of the smelliest bin lorry and you're still not close to how smelly those squirrels were.

Have you ever seen a squirrel taking a bath?

Exactly.

Still, this was an emergency, so through the door I went. It had to be me because Carrie and Laurence don't speak Squirrel. Embarrassingly, I got a bit stuck in the door – mostly because it was an extremely small door. It was designed for squirrels, after all.

Laurence and Carrie gave me a shove. It was very undignified. And then those pesky squirrels shouted **"Chunks"** again, which I told them they could stop doing now because we had heard them.

I established that Dorothea wasn't down here – she was still above ground – so I spoke to a squirrel called Janet. Janet was one of those types who close their eyes when they're talking to you, as if they

can't bear to look you in the eye. Maybe she was shy. She explained that Spruce Motel had called an emergency meeting earlier on, just as they were gathering for tonight's important work. They had suspected something strange was going on because they'd never had an emergency meeting before.

He'd called them into this room and said Father Christmas had some special instructions he wanted to pass on to them.

However, as soon as they were all inside, Spruce slammed the door shut and locked it. He offered no explanation and no apology. And no instructions from Father Christmas either.

They'd all started chanting **"chunks'** because it means **"help"** in Squirrel. I knew that already,

I explained to Janet, because I talk Squirrel, otherwise how could I be talking to her now?

Honestly! Squirrels! Not the brightest.

I asked Janet what the squirrels wanted to do now that we'd got the door open, hoping she'd say that they wanted to have a nice bubble bath and shampoo. But she said they'd better go and deliver the presents, as that was what they were meant to be doing.

No sooner had I said, **"OK – well, you'd better get on with it,"** than Janet gave a signal and all one thousand squirrels made a dash for the exit. If being smelly and not too clever are issues for squirrels, then let me add rudeness to that list. They barged past me without so much as a **"please"** or an **"excuse me"** or a **"thank you"**. Shocking, their lack of manners. Shocking.

Chapter Twenty-Nine

Laurence

Carrie and I were outside the room when every squirrel charged for the door. I rolled out of the way and gave a shout to Carrie, who stepped aside. A squirrel stampede.

They poured out of the little door, half heading one way and half the other. It was a blur of squirrel fur and squirrel tails and the tippety-tappety sounds of their long finger and toenails scrambling on the hard dirt floor. A frenzy for a minute, then silence.

Barrie emerged through the doorway and got stuck again. We pulled him out by grabbing his collar. He was followed by one last squirrel who closed her eyes, made some chattery noises in Barrie's direction and then ran off too.

Carrie stuck her head inside the little door.

"**Smells disgusting in there,**" was her only comment.

"**It does, doesn't it?**" said a voice from behind us. We turned to see Spruce Motel standing there, a big smile on his face.

"**Spruce!**" I blurted. Then I said, "**Mr Motel,**" in case calling an elf you don't know very well by their first name is rude.

"**I'm delighted to see the three of you down here again!**" he said. "**To what do I owe the pleasure?**"

"**You don't mind us being here?**" said Carrie.

"**Not at all! Always great to see you.**"

"**We thought you might be a bit busier tonight,**" I said, thinking we might as well get straight to the point.

"**How's that?**" he said, still with a broad grin on his face.

"**Well,**" I said, "**it's Christmas Eve and the night all the presents get delivered so...**" I trailed off. Surely it was obvious what I was getting at? But not to Spruce, it seemed.

"**So ... what?**" he said.

"**Why aren't you delivering presents?**" asked Carrie.

"**And where are the presents?**" I added.

"**What a lot of questions!**" said Spruce, throwing back his head and roaring with laughter. What exactly he was laughing at was a mystery to me.

I noticed, too, that he was keeping a wary eye on Barrie, who was staring hard back. The elf was definitely scared of him.

"**The Christmas operation is mysterious!**"

he said. "You don't expect me to reveal all of Father Christmas's secrets now, do you?"

Carrie frowned. "No ... but—"

"Precisely," Spruce said. "You two are going to have to trust me. Now it really is time for you to go home and get back into your beds. The one thing I can tell you is that no presents are ever delivered to a house unless it contains a sleeping child. You don't want to miss out!" Then he chuckled again.

"But why were there a thousand squirrels locked in that room?" I said. "Are you sure everything is OK? Our dog insisted we come down here again tonight and he would never do that without a good reason."

"He ... insisted?" asked Spruce. He was still smiling, but I got the sense he was working hard to keep that smile on his face.

"Yes."

"How did he 'insist', may I ask?"

"He pulled us out of bed and took us to the postbox," I told him.

"Right."

"But we couldn't get in that way so—"

"That's not important," Carrie interrupted. I instantly understood why. She didn't want to reveal to Spruce how we'd got down here.

"We're concerned about Christmas," she said.

"I'm touched by your concern," said Spruce, "but let me reassure you again – there is nothing to worry about. And those squirrels? Um, they locked themselves in."

"The squirrels locked themselves in?"

Spruce nodded. "That's right."

"How? The key was on the outside of the door."

"Squirrels are very clever."

"They might be clever," said Carrie, "but locking yourself in and leaving the key in the lock on the other side of the door... That's just not possible."

"These squirrels are special Christmas squirrels."

"And where are all the presents?"

"**GO HOME!**" shouted Spruce loudly and angrily. He gathered himself and added, "**Please,**" in a sweeter tone of voice.

Look, I get it. Carrie and I can be annoying. Everyone's annoying at one point. We ask a lot of questions and it sometimes makes Mum and Dad irritated too. If we don't understand something, then we'll ask questions until we do. Mum says we ask her *hundreds* of questions in a day sometimes and that, even though it annoys her, she's secretly pleased that we're so curious.

"**Being curious is the most important thing of all,**" she'd told us once.

"**But what about being alive? Surely that's the most important thing of all?**" I'd said, and Carrie had said, "**And what about love? You told us that was the most important thing of all, didn't you?**"

And then I'd said, "**And what about food? If you don't have food, then you die, so isn't that the most important thing of all?**"

And Carrie had said, "**Well, in that case, what about oxygen? Isn't that the most important thing of all?**"

And I had said, "**What about the universe? If there's no universe, then there's nothing, so isn't that the most important thing of all?"

And Mum had said she wished she hadn't said anything in the first place.

So I got that we were being annoying, but nothing here was making sense and we wanted to know why. There was *definitely* something Spruce Motel wasn't telling us. It seemed as though he wanted us to go away and leave him alone, which was suspicious. And he wasn't delivering any presents, which was suspicious too, because this *was* Christmas Eve.

"The thing is," I said, "I asked Father Christmas for a new bike and there was nothing by our tree and there are no presents down here and—"

"Oh, I see!" said the elf triumphantly. "At last the truth comes out! You're only worried about your own gifts. You're only pretending to worry about Christmas and the other children, but really all you can think about is yourself!"

"That's not true!" I protested. "It's just an example."

"Oh, how convenient!" scoffed Spruce. "How convenient that the only example you give is your own present!" Which made me feel like I was being selfish, but it really was only an example.

"You're changing the subject, Spruce," said Carrie, and I thought, *Yes, he* is *changing the subject – thank you, Carrie!*

Barrie nudged me with his nose. I looked down at him and he glanced to his right. I followed his gaze and saw what he was trying to point out to me – that the squirrels were back. *All* the squirrels, it seemed.

They were walking slowly towards us down the tunnel, from both sides, in complete silence. I felt the hairs standing up on the back of my neck.

Squirrels dashing here and there or eating nuts quickly or climbing things: fine. Squirrels slowly and quietly and deliberately walking towards you: frightening.

They had their eyes fixed on Spruce, but I couldn't tell whether that was because they were awaiting instructions from him (like **"Kill these children!"**) or whether they were out to get him. We were trapped either way. They were blocking the only two routes out of here. Barrie let out a low growl.

Spruce noticed the squirrels too. If he was worried, he didn't show it.

"Ah," he said to them in a loud voice. **"Squirrels, you are back. Good."**

One of the squirrels at the front closed his/her eyes and chattered away for a moment.

"Yes, completely," said Spruce. I wish I spoke

Squirrel. "**I understand what you are saying. I understand completely. And you're in luck because I have just spoken to FC and have an important update for you.**"

"**FC is Father Christmas,**" I whispered to Carrie.

"**I know,**" she whispered back. "**I'm not an idiot.**" Which I thought was a bit harsh, but we were both under a lot of stress.

"**Now,**" said Spruce, turning from one group of squirrels to the other, "**it'll be easier to talk to you if you're all in one place. I fell off a sleigh the other day and hurt my neck, so looking from one side to the other like this is difficult for me. Would you mind all lining up over here on the right for me?**"

Spruce rubbed his neck – he looked in pain. The squirrels had a quick chat between themselves and must have decided that they didn't mind because all the squirrels to the left of us moved to join all the squirrels to the right of us. A couple of them stared at us as they passed, but for the most part it was as if we weren't here. They certainly looked solemn and serious, although I don't hang out with loads of squirrels normally, so it was a little difficult to tell. Maybe all squirrels look solemn and serious up close.

Once the squirrels were standing together, Spruce turned to face them.

"**So,**" he said, taking half a step backwards, "**FC just sent me a message.**"

He took another half-step backwards.

"**A message that I think you're going to find very interesting.**"

He took another half-step back.

"In fact, this message from FC will clear up all the questions and concerns that you have about what has been happening here both tonight..."

He took a bigger step back.

"... and indeed what has been happening over the last few weeks."

Another step back.

"What FC said was..."

Another step.

"Now, please pay close attention because this is important..."

Another step.

"What he said was..."

Another step.

"Are you sure you are listening carefully?"

And Spruce Motel turned and ran away as fast as his little legs could carry him.

Chapter Thirty
Carrie

I thought it was pretty obvious that Spruce was going to make a run for it as soon as he took one step backwards. If you're really trying to engage with people (or squirrels), you move *towards* them, not away from them. His body language gave away what was actually going on in his head.

I have to say that I think of myself as a bit of an expert in the subject of body language, although Laurence doesn't like me talking about it because he says it makes him self-conscious about his arms and legs and his body. I didn't really understand how, but I stopped bringing it up with him. It still feels like a useful skill to have, though, and I think it would have served the squirrels well in this situation. Sure, Spruce was *saying* all the right things, but his body was telling a different story. Body language doesn't lie.

Examples: crossing your arms can mean you're trying to protect yourself or you're feeling defensive (unless you're just cold and trying to warm up), and avoiding looking someone in the eyes can mean you're lying or nervous, while slouching is a sign you're bored or tired, and fidgeting can show you're anxious.

When we first met Spruce, I noticed that he smiled a lot, but his smile was only really with his mouth. His eyes weren't smiling, so I reckon he was faking it. Most people fake a smile occasionally, like if your friend tells you a really bad joke but you don't want to be rude or hurt their feelings so you pretend to smile, or you meet someone for the first time and are smiling but distracted.

Anyway, I didn't write Spruce off completely, but I noticed his eyes didn't match his smiling mouth, and when he started moving backwards while saying that he was going to give the squirrels some news, I immediately thought, *There's something going on here!* I guess some people have a feel for it and others don't.

Most of the squirrels set off in pursuit of Spruce, who, it turned out, was an incredibly fast runner. He was *out of there*. I reckon he'd be in with a shot of a gold medal at the Olympics – that is, if they changed the rules and allowed elves to enter. Squirrels are quick, but Spruce moved so fast that I doubted the squirrels would have much of a chance.

Two of the remaining squirrels rushed up to Barrie. One of them closed her eyes as she chattered in Squirrel at him. Closing your eyes when you talk can mean lots of things, but it can indicate you're hiding your true feelings. So I kept that squirrel in my sights.

Anyway, after a few seconds of this, the two squirrels leapt on to Barrie's back and he headed off in the direction of the other squirrels. They rode off on him as if he was a horse and they were jockeys!

Laurence and I were now alone. We exchanged a look and shook our heads in amazement. We were both thinking the same thing: *We might as well follow everyone else.*

So we did.

Chapter Thirty-One

Barrie

I didn't mind helping out. I even didn't mind carrying a couple of squirrels on my back.

Yes, I was concerned about where they'd *been*. Squirrels are filthy animals.

Yes, it annoyed me that Janet, sitting furthest forward, had grabbed my fur in her paws and was yanking it like reins on a horse, trying to steer me right and left. I knew where I was going, for goodness' sake! Straight down the tunnel after the elf!

Yes, the squirrel at the back (I hadn't caught its name) dug its claws into my skin when we went round corners and that hurt, but I accepted that it was probably just trying to hang on and not fall off, so I said nothing.

I could put up with all that. But then after begging for a ride (**"We'll never catch Spruce without you!" "Please, you're our only hope!" "You're so big and strong!"**...) and them explaining that Christmas was in trouble if we didn't catch the elf, and me agreeing and saying, **"Jump on"**, what really irritated me was that they then sat on my back as I did all the work and discussed what they should do next and talked about me as if I wasn't there!

"We could get the dog to threaten him," said not-Janet.

"Yeah, the dog will have to get all heavy with the elf. Maybe even bite him if it comes to that."

"Do you think the dog is clever enough to pull this off?"

And I'm thinking, *Excuse me! I'm right here! Stop talking about me as if I can't hear you, and stop assuming I'll do whatever you command me to!*

It was rude.

I didn't say anything, though, as I was too busy trying to catch Spruce. We were catching up with the other squirrels. Squirrels are quick – quicker than me over short distances definitely – but they tire quickly. No staying power. So before long I was surging past squirrels who couldn't hack it and had dropped to a slow jog.

"KEEP TO THE RIGHT!" I barked. I nearly stepped on a couple who were strolling down the middle of the tunnel like they owned the place. Honestly! Squirrels!

Soon I'd passed every squirrel and it was just me against Spruce. I could see him in the distance, his little arms and legs pumping up and down for all they were worth, but I knew I had the beating of him. We St Bernards may be big but we're total athletes. It's bred into us. We can't lose it.

Having said that, I was feeling a bit wheezy at this point, so I hoped the elf was going to tire out. It had been a huge rush of adrenaline when I first took off after him, but now it was becoming a slog.

My naturally brilliant sense of direction told me that he seemed to be going in a big loop. I was pretty sure we were turning left a lot more than we were turning right. If these tunnels ran underneath every road in our neighbourhood, then I thought we could end up back where we started.

"It's quite comfy up here," I heard Janet say to her mate on my back. **"We should ride this dog more often."**

"I HAVE A NAME!" I barked crossly. **"This**

dog is called Barrie, so please use my name, thank you."

There was silence from my back. I bet they were looking at each other and rolling their eyes or sniggering.

Rounding the next corner, I was surprised to find that Spruce had stopped running and was trying frantically to open a small door in the wall. He had a bunch of keys and was trying one after the other in the lock. His hands were shaking.

Janet pulled hard on the hairs on my back and said, **"WHOA!"**

I found that so annoying that I slammed the brakes on, and she and her mate went flying into the wall. *Of course* I was going to stop.

"I'M NOT A HORSE!" I barked, but I was so out of breath it came out a bit limply and sounded like I was saying, **"I'm indoors,"** which would have been a weird thing to say at that point.

Spruce tried another key in the lock. I had no idea what was in that room, but it felt important to stop him from going inside, so I moved towards him, growling. I fully intended to start barking at him too, but I needed to get my breath back first.

The squirrels had got to their feet by now and Janet said, **"Don't let him open that door!"**

I wanted to tell her that I'd worked that out already, thanks very much, but I figured that could wait. So I growled a bit more at Spruce and was able to manage a couple of barks too, although I was still really out of breath.

I'm normally fast asleep at this time of night.

Chapter Thirty-Two — Laurence

Barrie's bark echoed through the tunnels. It didn't seem like he was very far away.

Carrie and I had been walking silently, feeling lost and anxious. As soon as we heard the bark, we ran towards the sound. It was a strange breathy bark, but it was definitely Barrie. Which was a relief. I think both of us were wondering whether we'd ever see Barrie again and whether we were going to be stuck down here in these empty, spooky tunnels for the rest of our lives.

When we got to him, Barrie was standing in front of the elf, barking. There were two squirrels nearby, chattering away. Spruce looked terrified.

"**You've got to help me,**" he pleaded, and I noticed he was crying. "**Please, call off your dog! If I can't get into this room, then Christmas isn't going to happen! Please!**"

Carrie had walked up to Barrie and was scratching his back. That always calmed him. She bent down and spoke into Barrie's ears.

"**It's all right,**" she said. "**It's all right, Barrie. Everything's all right.**"

Barrie stopped barking.

"**We don't know whether to trust you,**" I said to Spruce. "**You just ran away. That makes you look guilty.**"

"**Yes, I know,**" said Spruce between sobs. He was really upset. "**The truth is that I've made a couple of mistakes and I need to put them right if Christmas is going to happen, but I can't tell** the squirrels what the mistakes were because they involve top-secret information and FC would be furious if that information got out. I felt it would be too hard to explain that to the squirrels, so I was hoping to slip off and sort everything out. But your dog was so fast that he caught up with me before I managed to get into the FC Room." He pointed to the door behind him. "So please can you let me get into this room, sort everything out and then I can give everyone a proper honest explanation?"

"What if you're lying?" I said. "What if we let you get into that room and ... something bad happens? Or you do something bad?"

"Then come in with me," said Spruce, starting to cry even harder. "I have nothing to hide, but please decide quickly. We have very little time left..."

I looked to Carrie. I was thinking we should give Spruce a chance. Carrie seemed less convinced.

"Only if Barrie comes too," she said. That was a good idea; Carrie must have noticed that Spruce was clearly frightened of Barrie.

"Yes, fine," said Spruce. **"Thank you."**

He wasted no time in finding the right key. The door unlocked, and he put his hand on the handle to open it.

"Wait!" Carrie said. **"Laurence and I go in first, then you, then Barrie."**

"Fine," said Spruce tetchily.

The two squirrels started chattering away before Barrie silenced them with a growl.

Carrie opened the door slowly and peered into the room.

"It's very dark in there," she said.

"I think the light's broken," said Spruce.

"Want me to go first?"

"No," Carrie snapped, before adding, "No thank you."

She slid into the dark room and held the door open for Spruce and me to follow.

"Stay with him, Laurence," she said. "Something about this room is strange."

I did as she asked, but was thinking, *It's just a room, Carrie. What can a room do?*

It was indeed pitch-black inside.

"I'm just going to close the door," said Spruce, grabbing the handle and pulling the door shut.

"Wait for Barrie..." began Carrie, but the door clicked and there was a flash of white light so intense it forced me to close my eyes and lift my hand to shield them.

When I opened them a second or two later, the first thing I noticed was the moon, shining brightly above us in the cloudless sky. The moonlight bounced off the snow that we were standing on, snow that stretched as far as could be seen in every direction. Spruce stood on an enormous sleigh pulled not by reindeer but a dozen huskies, who, when they saw us, threw back their heads and howled mournfully into the black night.

Chapter Thirty-Three
Carrie

I had known there was something odd about that room the moment I opened the door. I couldn't tell what exactly – it was just a feeling I'd had, but a feeling so strong it was like being slapped in the face. It was as if the room crackled with electricity. It was powerful.

So, even though I had no idea what was going to happen, I knew *something* would. I felt it deep in my bones. But it was still a shock to end up out there in the snow and the moonlight.

"**You should get in this sleigh,**" Spruce shouted above the yowling of the dogs, his voice now cold and hard. "Because I'm about to drive away and I reckon you don't want to be left out here to freeze."

"Is Barrie all right?" I said. "If anything happens to that dog, I swear—"

"I haven't done anything with him," said Spruce. "I'm leaving in a sec, so I suggest you get in this sleigh."

Laurence didn't move, so I gave him a shove and we climbed on board. What choice did we have?

There was a low bench at the back and Laurence sank on to it, staring glassily at the elf and the flat, featureless landscape around us. The pack of dogs howled some more and snarled angrily at us.

"Where are we?" I asked, but Spruce didn't answer.

Instead, he shouted a command that I couldn't

make out, and the dogs stopped howling and leapt into action. They strained forward and, slowly at first, the sleigh began to move. Soon we were zipping along, the sleigh jumping and jolting across the hard snow.

Laurence sat stiff and still beside me, looking worried. I reached out and did something I don't think I've done since we were little: I held his hand. I'm not sure he even noticed, but it made me feel a bit better.

"**Excuse me, Spruce,**" I shouted, trying to be heard over the wind and the noise of the sleigh scraping the ice and the panting of the dogs. "**Where are we? What's happening? Why are we here?**"

But Spruce didn't turn round or acknowledge that he'd even heard me.

I tried to think clearly without panicking.

Easier said than done, because I could feel panic starting to rise inside me.

OK.

Where were we?

I looked around. Flat snow stretched out in all directions. Were we… Could we be … at the North Pole? I felt ridiculous for even thinking it. How would it be possible to jump from a tunnel under our little neighbourhood to the North Pole in an instant? But the world was no longer the place I had always imagined it to be. There were elves, for starters, and organized squirrels, and tunnels with doors under the streets I had innocently walked along my whole life. There had been this other reality without me ever knowing about it, so close to the world I knew.

So why couldn't there be a way of transporting us to the North Pole? It was hard to argue with the facts: seconds ago we'd walked into an underground room and now we were sitting at the back of a sleigh, a sleigh being driven by an elf ... and it was becoming increasingly hard to ignore that I was bone-chillingly *freezing*.

I looked at what we were wearing. We had dressed for a cold night in winter in Britain, not for a cold night in winter in, possibly, *the Arctic*. It was becoming clear pretty quickly that there was a difference. A big difference. This place was so cold it hurt.

I took Laurence's other hand in mine and he turned to me at last, but it was as though he wasn't quite there. There was a lost, faraway look in his eyes.

"**Are you OK?**" I asked him. He didn't reply. "**Come on, I can't do this on my own,**" I begged. "**Please.**"

Over his shoulder, way off in the distance, I could make out buildings. Lots of small houses. Smoke was rising from chimneys, and there were street lights glowing a dirty yellow. A village? Warmth! Shelter!

I expected our sleigh to turn and head towards them, but Spruce didn't even glance over. Soon we had driven further into the darkness, and the group of houses and buildings faded into the distance until I could no longer see them.

I tried to remember what I knew about huskies. I had done a project about them at school a couple of years ago, so I knew a fair bit.

They're able to live outside all day and all night, all the year round. And the outdoors here, if we were indeed inside the Arctic Circle, gets down to -40°C. That's *minus* forty. They are so tough.

My cousin Michael who lives in Ireland has a

husky called Benjamin P. Benjamin and once when I was about six he barked suddenly in my face (Benjamin P. Benjamin, not Michael) and it scared me silly. Michael loves Benjamin P. Benjamin and says he wouldn't hurt a fly, but I've been frightened of huskies ever since, which I know is probably not logical, but we don't always behave logically, do we? This wasn't helping my mood *at all*. I tried to stop thinking about huskies and Bejamin P. Benjamin.

"**Spruce works for Father Christmas,**" I said to my brother. "**He can't be bad. He won't let any harm come to us, will he?**"

Laurence said nothing, so I gripped his hand tighter.

Chapter Thirty-Four

Barrie

I sat and waited patiently outside the door for a long time.

A *long* time. That's what we dogs do. We wait for our owners. We are loyal.

It's hard sometimes knowing when to be patient and when not to be. I shouldn't have been quite so patient outside the door. I should have tried to get in there earlier.

The squirrels started making fun of me almost straight away. That's the thing about squirrels – not very bright. When they should have been worrying about what Spruce was up to in that room, all they could do was make jokes about me.

"Your friends couldn't wait to get away from you!" one said.

"My friends are my pack," I replied. "We look out for each other."

"Try brushing your teeth occasionally and they might want to hang out with you," said another.

"Of course they want to hang out with me," I said. "We're a team."

"Sit!" said another, laughing. "Good boy! Sit!"

Squirrels think it's hilarious that we dogs are told to sit and stay and fetch and lie down by our owners and that we obey them. They're always teasing us about it. In the park, they often shout "Sit!" at me as I'm walking past. It's infuriating.

Squirrels reckon they are so cool because they'd never do what they were told by anybody, especially not humans. I pointed out they were doing what Father Christmas told them to do, so maybe they weren't as cool as they thought. Didn't stop them laughing at me, and soon there was a whole crowd of them watching me waiting outside the door, all making sarcastic comments.

I snarled at one of them and it made him jump, which pleased me, but then he said I couldn't take a joke, and the rest of them began discussing how dogs have no sense of humour, which isn't true.

Eventually, after waiting for quite a long time, I started barking. But the door remained closed. Thing is, I knew Laurence and Carrie would never forget about me. If they weren't coming out of that room, there must have been a very good reason.

I tried turning the handle, but it was one of those round ones and I couldn't do it. I sat back down and, as I did so, about a hundred of the squirrels said, **"SIT!"**

So annoying.

Laurence and Carrie weren't coming out. Had they gone somewhere? I suddenly felt very alone.

"People who go into that room don't come out again," said one of the more helpful squirrels. "We can try to open the door but I wouldn't go in there on your own if I were you."

That's it! I thought. *This will be easier if I'm not alone. I need help.*

I turned to the squirrels and said, "I need you to do me a favour."

Chapter Thirty-Five: Laurence

After a journey that felt like it would never end, we rounded a small hill. There on the other side of it was a single building. The dogs pulled up to it and stopped.

Spruce walked over to the door, but there was so much snow piled up in front of it that he had to clear it before it would open. It took him several minutes and I was becoming seriously worried about Carrie surviving in this cold. I did my best to try to keep her warm, but I was shaking too. I suggested we do some star jumps to warm up, but Carrie just shook her head.

After what felt like an age, Spruce cleared the door and forced it open.

"**Come on!**" he yelled. So we staggered over and into the building.

It was a relief to get out of the wind, but it wasn't much warmer inside. It was one big room stacked from floor to ceiling with hundreds of wrapped presents. Could these be *our* Christmas presents and the presents of the other children in our neighbourhood? Had Spruce hidden them here for some reason? But why would he do that?

The elf set to work at the fireplace and soon had a fire blazing in the hearth. He disappeared out to his sleigh while Carrie and I waited for the heat from the fire to revive us. We were exhausted. The cold really saps your energy. Outside, the huskies began to howl. At what, I have no idea, but the sound spooked me.

I wondered if Spruce was going to leave us here and drive off, but after a few minutes the door opened again and he came in carrying an armful of packets and tins.

He threw them on to the table by the door as we stared at him, too cold and hungry and tired to know what to do. At least, that's how I felt, so I assume Carrie felt the same.

Spruce turned to walk out again.

"Wait!" I said to him. **"You're leaving?"**

"Yes," he said. **"There's enough wood to keep the fire going – don't let it go out. And there's food here. I'll be back soon. You'll be fine. Wait here for me. Eat, keep warm. Merry Christmas."**

"But where are you going?" I asked. **"Where are we? Where's Barrie?"**

"No questions," he said briskly. **"I have things to do."**

He turned to leave and I heard a sob from Carrie next to me – and that was it. I crumbled too. I started to cry. More than cry. I completely lost it. This all felt so hopeless and frightening and confusing. Could anyone blame us for feeling like this? We were cold, tired, confused, lost, desperate, and we were about to be left alone here in this abandoned cabin in the middle of nowhere. Worse than the middle of nowhere – in the middle of the Arctic or the Antarctic or Siberia or wherever we were. A vast, bleak snow-filled wilderness, apart from that small group of buildings we'd seen in the distance at one point.

In my mind's eye I was suddenly above the building we were in, looking down on it. The cabin was a dot in a sea of white, getting smaller and smaller as I pulled back and up to reveal more and more emptiness around us. An ocean of nothingness.

The mental picture made me cry harder, which set Carrie off even more.

"Stop crying!" said Spruce, looking alarmed. **"Stop it!"**

But we couldn't. The tears came hard and fast. Soon we were roaring, overcome with distress. You could hear the dogs outside respond by howling back. I wailed, Carrie wailed, the huskies howled. It seemed to upset Spruce, who became agitated, hopping from foot to foot.

"Stop it!" he shouted. **"Stop crying!"** He put his hands over his ears to blot out the sound, but it can't have worked. **"I'm going!"** he said. **"Your crying won't make any difference to that!"**

And he turned and left.

This made us more upset. We screamed in anguish, lost to our hopelessness.

Seconds later, Spruce was back.

"I SAID STOP IT!" he bellowed. He was trying to sound stern, but he couldn't disguise the worry he was clearly feeling. **"Look, if you stop crying, I'll explain what's going on."**

We gulped and snorted and squirmed, trying to calm down. It helped a bit that the fire was warming up the room so it began to feel a little less bleak. Feeling was coming back to our fingers and toes, which had gone numb. I shuddered as I struggled to breathe normally, but the panic was winding down. I was coming back to myself.

"That's better," said Spruce. **"For goodness' sake. Honestly!"** He sounded gruff but I could tell he was concerned.

"Tell us what's going on with the squirrels,"

Carrie said. "And the presents. And Christmas. And what are these mistakes you've made that you need to put right?"

Spruce took a deep breath. "Delivering the presents was my job," he said. "It was my father's job before me, and his father's job before him. For as far back as anyone can remember it has been the job of the Head Elf. I am now the Head Elf, so it should be my job.

"But a few years ago Father Christmas decided to start using squirrels. FC told me that not much would change, but it has. Every year, the squirrels do more and more and I do less and less. They started off delivering presents to a handful of houses, and this year they're delivering presents to your whole neighbourhood. If it goes well, next year they'll deliver presents to half the country, and then

FC will start using other animals around the world. I'll be out of a job. It's demeaning. It's humiliating. And it's happening on my watch.

"I will go down in history as the elf who let squirrels take his power and his dignity and, because of that, the power and dignity of all elves. I will go down in history as the world's biggest loser. I can't let that happen. When my plan works tonight, FC will realize what a disaster it is using squirrels to do an elf's job, and things will return to normal. Everything will be better next year."

"You locked the squirrels up so they couldn't deliver presents!" I said.

"And you're keeping the presents here," said Carrie, "so that Father Christmas will think they've failed. None of the children in our neighbourhood will get their presents tonight."

"That's unfortunate," said Spruce, "but it can't be helped. The only fly in the ointment was you two and your dog, so I need to keep you out of the way until Christmas is over."

"Where's Barrie?" said Carrie. "What have you done with him?"

"Nothing," said Spruce. "He'll be where we left him. He'll be fine. Now, I can't stand here talking to you all night. I have to go and watch the squirrels fail and Christmas fall apart. Goodbye. See you in a couple of days."

Before we could say another word, he turned and ran out of the door.

Chapter Thirty-Six
Barrie

"**Are you ready?**" Janet said to me, paw on the handle of the door marked "**34**". As usual, she had her eyes closed as she spoke to me. The door would lead, or so Janet had promised me, into Rocky Hamilton's house.

"**Yes,**" I said quietly. "**Go!**"

Janet opened the little door and I crawled through the narrow opening, expecting to emerge into a cellar because that's where the door to the tunnels had been in our house. Instead, I was surprised to find myself in a room with a vacuum cleaner, an ironing board and a broom. It was cluttered. The sloping ceiling told me I must be in a cupboard under some stairs.

As gently as I could, I pushed open the cupboard door with my nose, trying desperately not to knock anything over and alert the house's sleeping occupants. The door opened on to a hallway, a hallway I recognized. I had been in this house before.

I knew Rocky slept in a basket in the kitchen, so I turned left and headed down a couple of steps, my nails tapping on the tiled floor and my breathing the only sounds.

Sure enough, there was Rocky, fast asleep in his grotty basket. This was the tricky bit: how to wake him without setting him off barking.

I blew gently on his face. He twitched but didn't wake up.

I carefully gave his nose a little poke with mine. Nothing.

I licked his right ear, oh-so gently.

"Rocky," I whispered. **"Rocky, wake up!"**

He opened one eye and looked at me for a second or two, then, as if his brain had finally caught up with what he saw, he sat bolt upright and I could tell he was about to bark.

I leant right into his face. **"It's all right,"** I said. **"It's just me. Barrie. Merry Christmas. I need your help. Don't bark!"**

And he didn't. He did breathe out dramatically, which was unfortunate, as it meant a mouthful of his sour breath wafted over me – but that was a small price to pay, I thought, as I retched slightly.

"We have to round up some of the others," I said. **"There's a squirrel called Janet waiting for us through a door inside the cupboard under your stairs. She'll take you to Daphne's house."**

Rocky looked confused. Understandably.

"Come on," I said. **"I'll explain as we go."**

Chapter Thirty-Seven
Carrie

Of course the first thing I did when Spruce left was run to the door, to try to follow him. But the door was locked. Laurence just stared at me as I rattled the handle a few times, desperately hoping it would open but knowing it was useless.

I banged on the door and shouted, **"SPRUCE!"**

I heard the elf shout a command at his huskies and then there was silence. They had gone.

I pressed my ear to the door and listened but could only make out the freezing wind whipping across the snow.

I decided to look for another way out. By the front

door were pegs on the wall, on which hung an old tatty oilskin coat. Off to the right was a door, so I ran to it. Inside was just a small bathroom.

That was it. The big room we were in had the fireplace, a sofa and two chairs. There were windows but none of them opened. The rest of the space was filled with stacks and stacks of wrapped Christmas presents.

We were prisoners.

"Well?" said Laurence, but I didn't respond.

What could I say? That we were stuck in this hut and had no means of escape? That, even if we could get outside, it was -40°C out there and miles to the nearest buildings? That we had no means of getting anywhere except by walking, even if we could work out in which direction to walk? We'd never survive in those sub-zero temperatures.

I didn't want to say any of those things out loud,

because saying them out loud would make them more real. And things were real enough at the moment.

So I tried to look on the bright side. I tried to focus on the positives rather than the negatives. That was the way I tended to approach life, so why change now?

"We have food," I said. "We're warm. We don't seem to be in any danger. We have each other. Barrie is safe. I don't think Spruce means us any harm. He'll be back for us soon..."

"We're going to freeze," said Laurence, who didn't share my positive approach to life. "We're going to freeze and people are going to find our frozen bodies here in three hundred years' time and wonder what happened to these two children. They're going to wonder how the two children ended up in this cabin thousands of miles from home and no one will be able to work it out. The ice will perfectly preserve our bodies and we will become famous as the Lost Ice Children of the Arctic or wherever we are, and they will display us in museums and future generations of children will look at us and pity us."

"Oh, come on, Laurence," I said. "I don't think that'll happen." But I'm not sure I believed my own words.

"I wonder what it feels like to freeze," he said.

"Stop it!"

"I guess we're about to find out."

"No, we are not," I said. "Now, why don't I make us a hot drink?"

"Do we have a kettle?"

"Um..." I looked around. "No." I rummaged through the food Spruce had left.

"Would you like ... a sardine?" There wasn't

much here that I fancied. **"Or a slice of malt loaf?"**

"What's malt loaf?"

"It's a loaf made of ... malt," I said.

"No."

"Condensed milk?"

"What's condensed milk?"

"Milk that's been condensed, I guess."

"No. Why would you condense food?"

I sat down on the sofa and Laurence joined me. We sat in silence.

"We'll be OK, won't we?" I said after a while.

Laurence said nothing.

"Won't we?" I said again.

Chapter Thirty-Eight
Barrie

We met back in the tunnel. Rocky and Janet had fetched Daphne and Dougald. I'd got Dusty Cooper and Thunder Patterson.

Dusty was talking away excitedly in Portuguese and kept saying **"Feliz Natal"** to everyone.

Dougald was banging on about how he'd had his fur washed the night before and couldn't lie down on it until it was completely dry, otherwise it went all flat on one side. I made no comment. This was not the time to ask Dougald why he was so vain. We had a mission.

Rocky got the door open, so it was time to

enter the room that had swallowed up Carrie and Laurence. Dozens of squirrels were watching us. I decided to ignore them. I called the dogs into a huddle.

"**Listen, chaps,**" I said. "**This might be a dangerous mission but it's one we have to make.**"

The squirrels started chanting "**SIT! SIT! SIT! SIT!**" at us. Wow, squirrels are annoying!

"**I come from a long line of St Bernards,**" I said, raising my voice to be heard over the squirrels. "**Noble dogs whose mission has always been to find and rescue people in distress.**"

"**Can't hear you,**" said Daphne.

The squirrels chanted more loudly: **"SIT! SIT! SIT!"**

I tried again.

"The greatest St Bernard who ever lived—"

"SIT! SIT! SIT!"

"The greatest St Bernard—"

"SIT! SIT! SIT!"

"The greatest—"

"SIT! SIT! SIT!"

"Forget it," I said, sighing. **"Let's go."**

I wanted to tell them about the greatest St Bernard who had ever lived: Barry, who – two hundred years ago in Switzerland – had saved over forty lives and who'd had a statue erected in his honour. I wanted to inspire my friends and motivate them, but I couldn't be heard over the squirrels, so I ushered all five dogs into the dark room and closed the door.

Chapter Thirty-Nine
Laurence

"**Are you awake?**" I whispered to Carrie.

We had decided to get some rest, but I hadn't been able to sleep and felt annoyed that she'd been able to. It was partly because she had accidentally stolen the blanket, wrapping it round and round herself as she slept, gradually leaving me with nothing.

It was getting colder and there was nothing like feeling cold to make everything feel bleaker.

I looked at the fire; it was starting to die out. I thought about putting more logs on, but I worried that we'd run out. The pile of logs by the fire was big, but who knew how long we'd be here? Spruce had said two days, but could we trust him? I figured we should make the wood last as long as possible, so I turned over, wrapped my arms tightly around myself, and tried to sleep too.

Chapter Forty
Barrie

Thunder Patterson was the first to speak.

"Snow," he said quietly. "**I know this stuff. It's snow.** My first winter as a puppy, it snowed loads and I remember hopping through it in the park with my parents. Good times."

"Barrie?" said Daphne. "**Where are we?**"

"**I don't exactly know,**" I said. I tried to sound confident and in control, but I felt neither of those things. "Spruce has brought Laurence and Carric here, and we have to find them. The thing is, I come from a long line of proud St Bernards. We have been rescuing people for hundreds of years. The most famous St Bernard was called Barry – Barry with a 'Y' – and he lived in Switzerland two hundred years ago–"

"Sorry to interrupt," said Daphne, "but would you mind if we just got on with it? It's bitterly cold and, as much as I want to hear about Barry with a 'Y', I fear I'd freeze before you got to the end of the story."

I blushed, embarrassed. We were only a few seconds into this rescue mission and already I was making a mess of it.

"We're with you, buddy," said Rocky. "Tell us what to do."

"What's going on?" said Thunder, looking around. "Are we joining the army?"

"It's all good, old pal," Rocky said to him gently. "The boss is filling us in."

I could have licked him for showing me that support, such a thoughtful dog.

I noticed a clear set of tracks heading off into the distance. The tracks looked like they had been left fairly recently by several dogs and a sleigh. There were no other tracks visible in the moonlight so these must have been left by Spruce. They were the only clue I had. Hopefully they would lead us to Laurence and Carrie.

"Let's go!" I said. **"Follow me!"**

Chapter Forty-One

Carrie

I woke up when Laurence started talking in his sleep. Well, not so much *talking* as *shouting*. What he was saying didn't make a whole lot of sense, but it was something about squirrels and chocolate as far as I could tell. And I think he said **"fizzy lemons"** at one point. I didn't want to wake him, as he must have been as exhausted as me, but he was stopping me from sleeping, so it was annoying.

It had also become much colder in the cabin and I noticed that the fire had gone out. As quietly as I could, I got off the sofa and went to put another few logs on the fire. It was horribly cold. I've never lived in a house with a real fire, so I don't know how they work, but I guessed it was a matter of putting logs on and it would start up again.

I threw a whole load of wood on to the ashes in the hearth and ran back to the sofa and the blanket. My teeth were chattering.

I lay there, staring across the room at the fire, waiting for the flames to appear and for the room to get warm again.

Chapter Forty-Two
Barrie

I learnt something new that night: it is not easy to run in snow.

The tracks made by the dogs and sleigh were frozen, so they were bobbly and uneven. Every now and again I'd trip and fall. My face was crusted with snow.

But if you ran next to the tracks the snow was deep and, especially for the smaller dogs like Rocky, exhausting. So we stuck to the tracks made by the dogs who'd pulled the sleigh.

I tried to keep the pace up, but I didn't want to tire everyone out by running too quickly. After we'd been running for a while, I decided they were struggling, so I stopped to give them a break.

"**You all right, boss?**" said Rocky.

"**You look a bit peaky,**" said Daphne.

"**I'm ... fine,**" I said a couple of minutes later when I could speak. "**Absolutely ... fine.**"

Thunder lifted a leg and had a pee. We all watched as the snow turned yellow.

"**Right, when you guys are feeling ready, we can get going,**" I said.

"**We're good,**" said Dougald. "**Let's go.**"

"**Just give me a minute,**" I said, slightly irritated. I was still struggling to breathe.

Chapter Forty-Three — Laurence

I woke up because it was getting seriously cold. Carrie was asleep beside me. Through the window, I could see that it was still the middle of the night. I wondered when morning would come. It seemed to have been night for a very long time. But, of course, maybe it wasn't going to get light! If we really were somewhere near the North Pole and it was the middle of winter, then there are weeks when the sun doesn't rise *at all*. It could be dark for another two *months*!

That was not a thought that cheered me up. And it was super cold. I couldn't feel my fingers or toes.

The fire, I thought. *We should get the fire going again.*

"**What are you doing?**" mumbled a sleepy Carrie.

"**The fire,**" I said, my teeth chattering.

There were some logs in the grate, but they weren't alight. I held my hand over them to see if there was any warmth coming off them. There wasn't.

"**It's gone out,**" I said. "**How do we light it again?**"

"**Matches?**" mumbled Carrie.

Yes, matches. I looked around. Couldn't see any.

"**Have you seen any matches?**" I asked her.

She sighed and swung her legs off the sofa and stood up.

We both checked for matches. Slowly, calmly at first, but the longer we couldn't find any, the more worried we got and the more frantically we looked.

For five, ten, maybe fifteen minutes, we scoured that room. We searched high; we searched low. Under the sofa, up the chimney, on the top of the door frame – we searched *everywhere*.

Nothing.

We stopped and looked at each other.

We'd let the fire go out.

There was no way of getting it going again.

We were in deep trouble.

Chapter Forty-Four

Barnie

There were a cluster of houses and street lights off to the left in the distance. They were the only signs of life we had seen. Everywhere else was just snow, snow, snow. But what confused me was the fact that the tracks we were following did not lead towards those houses. They went off in a different direction, further into the darkness. What should we do?

I slowed and stopped.

"**Everyone feeling all right?**" I asked.

"**Good, boss,**" said Rocky. He was always so positive. I loved that about him.

"**Where are we?**" asked a bewildered Thunder.

Standing here in the bleak, cold darkness, I suddenly wondered whether I'd recklessly put everyone in danger. Was I leading them all to disaster? Should I have come on my own and not asked my friends to risk so much for me?

But it wasn't for *me*, was it? It was for Carrie and Laurence. And I knew that if any one of these dogs had asked me for my help, I would have been more than happy to give it. I tried to push negative thoughts out of my head. The way I could repay my friends' willingness to help me on this rescue mission was to make good decisions and not put them into any unnecessary danger.

So… *Should we carry on following the tracks or should we head for the houses?* I thought.

Daphne came over to me.

"Everything OK?" she said.

"Yes, Daphne. The tracks go this way, but

there are houses over there. I think we should carry on following the tracks because that should lead us to Carrie and Laurence, but maybe we should seek shelter. What if we're heading into danger? What if the weather gets worse and we're stuck out here?"

"We came here to find Carrie and Laurence, didn't we?" she asked, and I knew what she was getting at. She was right.

"**Come on, everyone!**" I called out, trying to sound confident. "**Let's go!**"

And with me leading, we followed the tracks as they snaked away into the darkness.

Chapter Forty-Five
Laurence

Carrie had noticed the oilskin coat by the front door. It was huge, big enough for an enormous man, which got us wondering who it belonged to. Not Spruce, that's for sure. You could have got three of him in that coat.

The fire was not going to light – we had accepted that. So we had to try to keep warm. We had no choice.

We had searched every corner of that room and found nothing useful.

Well, I found a harness for a sleigh, but what use is a harness without a sleigh? I hung it on a peg by the door. At one point we thought about opening all the stolen Christmas presents stacked from floor to ceiling, but not only did that feel very wrong (you should never, ever open someone else's present without their permission!) but we thought that Father Christmas wouldn't give a child a box of matches or a lighter as a present. Simply not going to happen.

We tried doing some star jumps to warm us up and that worked for a bit. We couldn't do star jumps for the next two days, though, could we?

We ate some malt loaf (which wasn't too bad), did a few more star jumps and then wrapped up together inside the oilskin coat and lay on the sofa.

"I let the fire go out," said Carrie sadly. "I'm so sorry."

"Don't worry," I replied. "It's just as much my fault. Anyway, it's Christmas. We'll be all right.

Nothing bad happens at Christmas, does it?"

She smiled at me, and I smiled back. I wasn't used to being the positive one, but I could see that what Carrie needed in that moment was hope. I shivered. And not only because I was cold.

Chapter Forty-Six
Barrie

The weather was getting worse. The wind had picked up and snow was starting to fall. I worried that the snow would cover the tracks we were following. Without those tracks, we were in terrible trouble. They were the only clue we had.

"Keep going!" I shouted. **"Nearly there!"**

I had no idea if that last bit was true or not, but it was better than shouting out, **"I have no idea where we are and if we'll ever find Carrie and Laurence!"** Or, **"I'm leading you into the unknown and I have no clue if we'll survive!"** No. That's not the sort of thing a good leader shouts.

But rounding a small hill ... I could see something! A building sitting all alone in the vast wilderness. And the tracks led up to it. This had to be where Carrie and Laurence were!

We ran to the door, Rocky jumping up and putting his paws on it. With all our tails wagging furiously, we barked and barked into the windy night.

I ran to the window and was just tall enough to see inside. The room seemed to be storage for Christmas presents. There were hundreds of them, piled right up to the ceiling.

But, in between two stacks of presents, there was a sofa and what looked like a big burrito lying on it. That had to be Carrie and Laurence! Perhaps they were wrapped in a blanket together?

Trouble was, they hadn't seen us and, despite us barking as loudly as we could, they didn't seem to hear us either. I scrabbled at the glass of the window with my nails. I barked. Nothing.

Dropping down, I ran towards the door. Apart from Dusty, the other dogs had descended into a frenzy of barking, and in my panicked state I joined

them. But Dusty stood there, looking around calmly.

On the step leading up to the door was a large stone. Dusty attempted to move it, pawing at it, trying to nose it out of the way. Neither worked. The stone was too big.

She barked something at me, which I couldn't understand but imagine was along the lines of **"Help me out"**.

I hurried over, and together we managed to roll the stone over and, there, underneath it was a key!

"Dusty!" I exclaimed. **"You genius!"**

She barked something that sounded like, **"My fish has a cold."** Once again, I cursed myself for not speaking Portuguese.

The other dogs had noticed what was going on and gathered round. Daphne picked up the key in her mouth and tried putting it into the lock. Not easy. Especially as she was so cold and shivering. She tried several times with no luck.

"Mind if I try?" said Thunder Patterson.

He was better than Daphne at holding the key in his mouth, but he was too short to reach the lock. So I lay down on my side and he climbed on to me. The ground was super cold, but I tried not to shake, as I knew that would make things more difficult for Thunder.

He tried a few times but kept dropping the key. I carried on lying there as he climbed down, got the key into his mouth at the right angle and tried again.

Then, at last, success! The key slid into the lock and we all cheered.

Trouble was, Thunder couldn't twist it in the lock to open the door. His whole body shook with the effort, but it wasn't happening. Everyone else, including me, had a go, but to no avail.

"I've got an idea!" said Rocky. **"Lie down again, Barrie. I'm the smallest, so I'll climb up and clamp my teeth hard on to the key, then I'll make my body as stiff as I can and you all turn me. If you turn me, you'll turn the key, and the door should open!"**

It was worth a go, I supposed, and no one else had a better idea, so we tried it.

Rocky clamped himself on to the key, then me and Daphne and Dougald pushed him round so that he would turn and the key in his mouth would turn too. The first time we tried it, Rocky let go immediately and dropped to the ground. He said we shouldn't push him under his armpits because he was ticklish.

We tried again – and it worked!

The lock clicked. I pressed down on the door handle and we were in!

Chapter Forty-Seven
Carrie

I thought I might be dreaming at first but, no, that was Barrie sitting on my head. He was wet and his fur was cold, but I've never been happier to see him. Laurence and I must have fallen asleep, so it was a shock to be woken by our big, beautiful Barrie suddenly jumping on to us.

Laurence and I were so tightly rolled up into the oilskin coat that it took a bit of struggling to free ourselves and, as we did so, I heard Laurence gasp. I looked over to see why, and there they were. Three dogs in a line staring at us, tails wagging.

"Hey, that's Thunder from across the road!"

I said. **"And Daphne! And Rocky!"**

"He's brought half the dogs in the street!" said Laurence. **"How did you find us, Barrie? How did you get here?"**

"How did they open the door?" I said.

It's at times like this that you wished dogs could speak so they could tell you what they'd been up to.

"Talking of doors," I said, and I got up to close the cabin door, which had been left open and was letting in an icy draught. As I went to it, Barrie followed and barked at me.

"It's like he doesn't want me to close the door," I said. **"It's freezing in here, Barrie, and having that door open is not helping."**

Barrie barked, and Daphne, the poodle from across the road, and Rocky moved to sit by the door.

"Are you expecting a delivery?" asked Laurence, which made me laugh.

Then Barrie nudged me back towards the sofa and pushed Thunder, the old dog with the sad eyes from the corner house, up on to the oilskin too. Barrie picked up the corner of the coat with his mouth and tried to drag it over us. He wanted Laurence and me to wrap up warm with Thunder. I didn't know if that was because he thought Thunder needed warming up or we did, but I didn't argue. Being out of our bundle for only a few minutes meant I was once again shaking uncontrollably with the cold. Laurence was too.

Thunder acted like a little hot-water bottle and it was nice cuddling up with him.

"We're waiting for Spruce to come back," I said to Barrie, even though he'd have no clue what I was saying. **"Did he bring you here? He must have. I am so pleased to see you."**

Barrie looked at us with his big eyes, then

turned and ran out of the door, followed by Rocky and Daphne.

It seemed as though he had some sort of plan, so Laurence and I, in our Thunder sandwich, pulled the oilskin tightly around us and tried not to think about how desperately cold we were.

Chapter Forty-Eight
Barrie

Once I'd got Laurence, Carrie and Thunder wrapped up together (because they all looked half-frozen), Daphne, Rocky and I ran outside, being careful to close the door behind us.

Dougald had had the clever idea to search around the building for a sleigh. If we wanted to get Carrie and Laurence out of here, we needed a sleigh. There was no way they'd be able to walk all the way back to those houses we'd seen. No way.

So Dougald and Dusty had gone looking together and they were barking excitedly for us to join them.

We found them round the side of the building,

standing over something big and almost completely buried in the deep snow. A sleigh! It had been very clever of Dusty and Dougald to notice it at all. I set them the task of digging it out because I had another job: finding the harness used for dogs to pull the sleigh. A sleigh on its own was no use at all because the ground was pretty flat. We had to be able to pull it.

The harness wasn't anywhere near the sleigh, so it must have been kept somewhere else. I thought I might be able to pick up the scent of the huskies who had once pulled it and find it that way. Huskies have a powerful and distinctive smell, and anything that had been used by them would surely still have their scent. Trouble was, the wind was so fierce it was hard to pick up anything.

Keeping my whole body as low to the ground as possible, I slowly made my way round the outside of the cabin, concentrating on picking up any whiff of husky. Anything outside would, by now, probably be buried quite deep in the snow. I remembered how much snow had been piled up against the door when we'd arrived.

I had no luck and found nothing.

The others had almost dug the sleigh out. I headed back into the cabin, again closing the front door behind me. It was a bit easier to think inside, away from that fierce wind. What was I going to do?

I closed my eyes and tried to imagine a solution to this issue of having a sleigh but no harness, and when I opened them again the answer was staring me in the face. And I mean literally staring me in the face – hanging from the coat pegs by the door was what looked like a sleigh harness.

I needed Laurence and Carrie to help. My paws had no chance with buckles and straps. I ran to the sofa and rubbed my face against Carrie's. She had been either asleep or maybe thinking with her eyes closed, but my snow-crusted face in hers soon brought her round. She looked at me blankly. This was not good. How could she be so sleepy at a time like this?

I clamped my teeth around her sleeve and pulled. She moaned my name. I pulled harder, and slowly she got to her feet.

Chapter Forty-Nine
Carrie

I followed Barrie outside. The other dogs were digging around a large object half covered in snow. I leant down and touched it with my gloved hand. It was a sleigh. A sleigh! Better than nothing, I suppose. We could sleigh to … well, to where?

I pulled and pulled, and the dogs kept digging. With a lot of pulling and digging and wiggling and the occasional shout of effort from me, we managed to drag it out from where it was buried. The sleigh was upside down. I flipped it over, nearly landing it on Rocky, who looked up at me as if to say, *Do you mind?*

Barrie was standing by the front door, barking at the pegs next to it. I looked over and, yes, hanging from them was the harness for the sleigh. Clever dog! He wanted to try to pull the sleigh. Could that work? Instead of huskies, we had Daphne the poodle, Rocky the terrier, Dougald the cockapoo, the mongrels Thunder and Dusty, and my big, beautiful Barrie, a St Bernard. It seemed unlikely. Frankly, it seemed almost impossible. But what choice did we have? I had no better plan.

I dashed to the pegs, grabbed the harness and ran outside with it. I had to find a way of attaching it to the sleigh. There were so many straps and buckles and the wind was howling and the snow was falling heavily…

I laid the harness in front of the sleigh, realized I had it back to front, so turned it round, then saw that I had it upside down, so flipped it over. Was that the right way round? I didn't want to spend ages trying to tie it on, only to find it was the wrong way round. I took off my gloves and began to try to attach it to the sleigh. Not easy. I had no feeling in my fingers at all.

Rocky was barking at me and I shooed him away. Maybe he was trying to be helpful, but he wasn't helping. The sound of his little bark was carried off into the distance with the wind. Off into the *empty* distance. Were we really going to head out into that dark wilderness?

My frozen fingers somehow managed to slide the last buckle into place.

"Barrie!" I called. **"Barrie, I did it. Come on!"**

Chapter Fifty
Barrie

I was inside checking on Laurence when I heard Carrie calling my name. I ran outside and found her standing with some of the harness in her hand.

I ran to the front of the harness, facing away from the sleigh, and stood still while she attached me. The other dogs stood watching from the hut – apart from Rocky, who stood next to Carrie, asking what he could do to help.

That's my friend, I thought proudly. *Good old Rocky.*

When I was buckled up, I told Rocky to get behind me and let Carrie tie him to the strings.

Trouble was, he was so excited he kept spinning round in circles and Carrie had to have a stern word with him. I told him to save his energy. We were going to need it.

I called out to Daphne to bring the others. She was bossy by nature and I figured she'd sort out the rest. And she did, slotting Dougald in beside Rocky, and Dusty and herself in the row behind.

Daphne and I decided it might be best if Thunder sat in the sleigh with Carrie and Laurence. But when we suggested that to Thunder, he walked into the next vacant slot without a word and stood waiting to be attached to the harness. It was such a brave and courageous gesture that I nearly wept.

Carrie ran into the cabin again and I expected to see her emerge with Laurence, but instead she came out with a pile of cushions, which she spread out on the floor of the sleigh. Then she went back inside.

The six of us stood silently waiting, all shivering in the cold. I noticed I was shivering less than the others and I felt a surge of pride. This was what I had been born to do. To protect and to rescue and to lead. Like my ancestors before me. Like Barry.

That pride soon turned to worry, though. It really was up to me now. I had to lead us to safety.

Laurence and Carrie emerged from the cabin at last.

They jumped into the sleigh, wrapped themselves up in the big coat, and we were ready.

Chapter Fifty-One — Laurence

"OK, Barrie!" I called. "Let's go!"

Barrie barked and the six dogs all started to run … but they ran in different directions and the result was that we didn't move. Not one bit.

Barrie barked. Daphne barked. Dougald barked. They all barked. This was hopeless.

Maybe if we got them going, they'd get the hang of it? I nudged Carrie, and we jumped up and ran to the back of the sleigh and started to push. It was heavy – no wonder the dogs were struggling. And it didn't help that the wind was howling right into our faces. We got as low as we could, gloved hands on the back of the sleigh.

The sleigh started to move forward, but it slid right into Thunder, knocking him clean off his feet.

"Sorry!" I called out. **"Sorry, Thunder!"**

He got up. All the dogs fell silent, except Daphne, who was doing lots of barking. It was as if she was giving them instructions. We pushed again, and this time we got the sleigh moving properly. The dogs all pulled in the right direction, and we were off and running!

I could have whooped for joy. In fact, I *did* whoop for joy. It was exciting. I punched the air. Carrie had already jumped aboard the moving sleigh and I ran to do the same.

But the dogs were getting the hang of it now and the sleigh was picking up speed. I ran as hard as I could, but the snow was deep, up to my waist, and I kept sinking into it and was only managing a kind of fast walk. Then I tripped on something and face-planted in a huge pile of snow.

I stood up, wiped the snow from my face … and watched in horror as the sleigh headed off into the distance without me.

"**STOP!**" I screamed, but the wind whipped my words into the night and no one heard me.

Chapter Fifty-Two
Barrie

It was tough. We were heading straight into the wind. But we got better and better, step by step.

Being at the front, a lot of it was up to me. I had to keep an eye out for obstacles, pick the best path. It wasn't easy, and I have to say I felt more and more respect for huskies with each stride.

I could hear Carrie shouting something behind us. Probably words of encouragement.

We were making steady progress. Well, we did for the first two minutes, until Rocky tripped and fell over. He completely lost his footing and slid on his back for a bit, his body acting like a brake on the sleigh. We ground to a halt.

"Everything OK, Rocky?" I asked.

"Yes," he panted. "**Sorry. Bit shorter than you. Deep snow. Sorry. Hold on.**"

"**You have your harness twisted,**" advised Daphne, standing next to him. "**You need to roll over.**"

Rocky did so.

"**No, not that way,**" Daphne said. "**Back the other way. It's twisted even more now. You'll have to do it twice the other way.**"

"**My fur is covered in icicles,**" said Dougald, even though no one had asked about his fur. Everyone ignored him.

We waited while Rocky sorted himself out. To be honest, I was glad of the rest. This was *hard work*.

"**Right,**" said Rocky. "**Got it. Sorry again. I'll try to do better.**"

I was about to give the command to set off again

when Carrie appeared next to me. She seemed upset. She kept waving her arms about.

"What are we waiting for?" asked Daphne.

"Don't know," I said.

What on earth was Carrie doing jumping off the sleigh? Maybe she needed to go to the loo. She stood next to me, holding the harness so I couldn't move.

I barked to let her know we needed to get going. I looked back and saw ... Laurence, breathless, climbing into the back of the sleigh. What was he doing? I glanced at Dusty and raised my eyebrows as if to say, *Humans!* Then Carrie went back to the sleigh and we were off again.

I was in charge of the direction we were going, but obviously I didn't know which way was correct. One direction just felt good, so that's where I headed. I can't explain it any better than that.

The falling snow had long since covered our

tracks from earlier, so I had no clues to go on – no landmarks, no signposts, no road. Only my gut instinct. The instinct developed in us St Bernards over hundreds and hundreds of years. The instinct passed from generation to generation, and on which I now based all our hopes of survival. Once I'd decided on a direction, all I could do was run and run. And I did. I ran my heart out.

Boy, was it difficult! I'm not ashamed to say that I cried a couple of times. There were several moments when I didn't think I could go on. I've never done anything as difficult in my life. I don't know how long we ran for. It felt like a lifetime, but maybe it was an hour. Maybe more, maybe less. All I could see was the snow immediately in front of me. All I could hear was the sound of my paws on the icy snow. The dogs behind me, so full of chat earlier, were talking no longer. I could hear the panting, the grunting, the effort they were making, and I burst with pride.

We dogs, working together, as a team, selflessly, were going to save Laurence and Carrie.

Barry would have been proud of us.

A sudden feeling of elation filled me, a surge of joy. Ecstasy flooded through my whole body. I was fulfilling my destiny! I was doing the thing I had been born to do! I was a St Bernard, and this was what St Bernards did!

I wondered if they would put up a statue to me one day. I pictured myself pulling a cord to reveal a big bronze statue of me and the other dogs, and hundreds of people clapping and the mayor putting a medal around our necks and Laurence and Carrie hugging me.

Suddenly the sleigh started to slow. It felt heavier. I turned and saw that Thunder had fallen.

"STOP!" I called.

Thunder, it seemed, had exhausted himself and would have to go into the sleigh with Carrie and Laurence.

Chapter Fifty-Three
Carrie

Once Laurence and I had untied Thunder and taken him into the sleigh with us, we could get back underway. The poor dog was shaking with tiredness. He had given everything he had.

Unfortunately, though, he was only the first dog to run out of steam. Things went smoothly for a bit, but then Dougald had to stop. Out we got, untied him, brought him into the sleigh and under the oilskin with us. Having two dogs in our little huddle was helping us to keep warmer, it had to be said.

But then Rocky had to give up, then Dusty. I couldn't blame them. The conditions were awful and they had tried so hard. Each time, we had to stop the sleigh, untie the dog from the harness with numb fingers, push the sleigh to start it going again, then jump in and try to keep warm.

Which was getting harder and harder. We were cold right through. It felt like our bones were freezing over. It was awful.

And as more dogs ended up in the sleigh, not only did we have fewer dogs pulling but the sleigh was getting heavier and more difficult to pull.

Barrie and Daphne were the only two left and did well for a while, battling hard to keep us going, but eventually Daphne slowed and stopped. She stood, head low, defeated.

That seemed to be that. There was no way Barrie could pull all of us on his own.

We brought Daphne into the sleigh to get warm, and then I went to untie Barrie. I didn't want to leave him on his own. The only thing we could do was huddle together as best we could until the dogs felt strong enough to have another go.

I knew what Laurence would be thinking and I was thinking the same: we were in deep trouble out here in this weather. But neither of us said anything. What was the point?

I reached Barrie, but he barked at me before I could untie him. I tried again, and he barked once more. He seemed to be telling me to stay away. I went back to ask Laurence to help when the sleigh started moving again. Barrie was pulling it on his own!

I jumped into the sleigh and watched with Laurence as our incredible dog, straining every muscle, trudged onwards. Head low, strong legs, big shoulders shaking with the exertion. Each step an awe-inspiring achievement. Each stride a miracle.

There were a few moments when it looked like he might stop, but each time he found new strength from somewhere and kept going. At one point, Laurence just jumped out of the sleigh to help push it and I followed. I don't know how much

help we were being, as we sank into snow and had to struggle out, but we weren't going to leave Barrie on his own.

So, little by little, we moved forward – a dog and two children in the huge wilderness of the Arctic and a sleigh of exhausted dogs.

Chapter Fifty-Four
Barrie

Just one more step.

Just one more step.

Just one more step.

Just one more step.

That was the only thing that went through my mind. Repeated over and over.

Just one more step.

I didn't want anything else in my head. I didn't want to think about stopping. I didn't want to think about the pain. I didn't want to think about the cold. I didn't want to think about Laurence or Carrie or Dusty or any of the other dogs. I didn't want to think about my nice warm bed. I didn't want to think about Mum and Dad. I didn't want to think about Barry.

Just one more step.

And I certainly didn't want to think about resting.

Just one more step.

If I gave space to anything other than *just one more step*, I wouldn't have gone on.

Just one more step.

Mind over matter.

Just one more step.

I didn't know where we were going or how long it would take or what was going to happen.

Just one more step.

I didn't know if it had been a mistake to leave the cabin.

Just one more step.

So, when three hundred squirrels came racing

through the snow towards us, I didn't take it in at first.

Just one more step.

I'm sure a part of my brain noticed them and thought, *Three hundred squirrels?* But the only thought that went through my head was:

Just one more step.

That many squirrels coming towards you across white snow in the moonlight looks like God has spilled a mug of coffee across his big white table. It looks like a brown wave about to crash on to the white shore. It looks like chocolate sauce spreading across vanilla ice cream. But I didn't think that at the time.

Just one more step.

And then the squirrels reached us and we could have been forgiven for thinking that they were some sort of mirage. Like when people starving in a desert see water where there isn't any, because it's the thing they crave so much that their brains conjure it up out of thin air.

Just one more step.

Although, just to be clear, squirrels were not what I was most craving at that moment.

They stopped, right in front of me. The squirrel at the front said, **"Hi,"** with her eyes closed and my next thought wasn't…

Just one more step …

… but …

JANET!

I stopped walking.

Janet stood, eyes closed, breathing heavily. It was her. It was definitely her.

Neither of us had the strength to speak.

Two squirrels stood directly behind her. Behind them stood three squirrels. Behind them, four. It seemed deliberate.

They seemed to be arranging themselves into rows. What were they doing?!

Behind the four stood five; behind them, six. I could only watch. When they got to about fifteen rows, only three squirrels formed the next row, and three behind them and three behind them.

I realized – they were making an arrow! A giant arrow pointing right at me!

And then I thought, *Why?*

Something caught my eye, flying high above.

I looked up, which – given my state – was more difficult than you might imagine.

Something big and travelling very fast whizzed past. The squirrels watched it intently. Even Janet had opened her eyes.

We stood there, silently gazing upwards at the now empty sky.

There it was again! Whizzing past in the opposite

direction. Three hundred squirrels followed its path.

Then it came in low and hard from the left. It landed silently and gracefully. A figure climbed out. A man. A man I knew.

"Hello, Barrie," he said. "**How nice to see you again.**"

I could only stand and stare.

"**Looks like you could do with a hand,**" he said.

Chapter Fifty-Five

Barrie

Laurence and Carrie don't know what happened next. How could they? They fell asleep as soon as Father Christmas arrived.

Children can't remain awake in his presence, but I'm sure you already know that. I don't know how it works. Children just fall straight to sleep. I know *why* – because you don't ever want a child seeing Father Christmas. Can you imagine what would happen? He'd never get anything done with all the questions they'd ask and the selfies and autographs and all the rest of it – but I don't know *how* he does it. He's Father Christmas. He does all sorts of stuff that I don't understand.

So let me fill you in.

Father Christmas asked one of his reindeer to help me out with pulling the sleigh. His reindeer are *huge*. I meet FC every Christmas when he drops the presents off for Carrie and Laurence, but he always leaves the reindeer and sleigh outside, so I hadn't seen them before. They are half the size of a house! Enormous!

FC went to the back of the sleigh and lifted Carrie and Laurence into it. FC said hi to a few of the other dogs that he

knows and introduced himself to the ones from houses that don't have children. He's polite like that. Good guy, FC.

Then one of those massive reindeer wrapped his antlers around the harness, ready to pull the sleigh.

FC asked me if I wanted to sit up with him and rest, but I said, **"No thanks – I've seen it this far. I want to finish the job."**

And he said, **"Of course you do. Wouldn't expect anything less."** Then he told me that I reminded him of Barry and, well, you can probably imagine what that did to me.

I was so exhausted and so relieved and so proud that he had said that – because he's the only person alive who knew Barry personally – that I started crying my eyes out as that big beefy reindeer and I dragged the sleigh full of the most precious children and dogs in all the world to safety.

Chapter Fifty-Six

Carrie

Laurence and I woke up in a dimly lit room. A dimly lit *warm* room. There was a huge fire burning in the hearth.

"**Soup?**"

A kindly-looking woman stood over us. Grey hair tied in a bun, small spectacles, a gap between her front teeth. Where was I?

"**Carrot soup?**" she said. "**We make it out**

of the carrots that the reindeer don't eat. Don't worry – we wash them first!" She laughed at her little joke.

I was starving, so I nodded. She clapped her hands and in through the door, carrying two bowls, walked Spruce Motel!

Laurence was awake now too, and we both eyed Spruce warily.

"Spruce has been a naughty boy," said the woman. "Haven't you, Spruce?"

"Yes, Mother Christmas," he said meekly.

"He's been punished, haven't you, Spruce?"

"Yes, Mother Christmas."

"He's been suspended from his job running the present-delivery operation because of what he did. At least until he can show he's come to his senses. It was a complete overreaction,

Spruce. There's no way Father Christmas would ever get rid of the elves. Never, never, never."

"I'm sorry," said Spruce to me and Laurence. "I'm so, so sorry for what I did. I'm sorry for taking you both and putting you in danger. It goes against everything I was taught as an elf. I feel awful. I got into such a muddle in my head. I was convinced Father Christmas was going to have no use for me any more because he had the squirrels. I got into a proper state. But it was all in my head. I should have just asked him."

"Spruce is going to help me out around the house for a while," said Mother Christmas. "We love him and all the elves. We thought the work was getting too much, so we wanted to help him out. Maybe we should have just asked too. Seems like a lot of wires got crossed."

Spruce nodded.

"Eat your soup," Mother Christmas said to us. "Then we have to get you home."

Chapter Fifty-Seven
Barrie

Dad took me for a walk on Christmas morning. He must have been amazed that Carrie and Laurence had slept so late. They'd never done that on Christmas morning before.

The first dog I ran into was Thunder, who looked tired but in remarkably good shape considering. He seemed to have a spring in his step that I hadn't seen in years – he was positively glowing.

"Good work, Barrie!" was all he said, and he said it several times. **"Good work! Good work!"**

Next, I bumped into Daphne, who said, **"I'm very impressed by you, Barrie."**

Well, that nearly started me crying with pride all over again. I didn't know what to say. I came over all shy and embarrassed. I mumbled something about a team effort and how we had all done our bit, gave her bottom one last sniff and headed off. I'm not used to praise.

Dusty was next, but I still couldn't understand a word she was saying. She was talking about toasters, I think, or it could have been hedgehogs. It was good to see her, though.

And then Rocky. He had lots of news. He'd seen Dorothea that morning and had some intel on what had happened last night.

Seems that after we dogs had gone into the dark room in the tunnels, the squirrels sat around talking. First of all, they'd talked about how annoying we dogs were and they all had a good laugh, but then one squirrel had said that she quite admired the way we'd worked together and our bravery in going into that room when we didn't know what was waiting for us. How we'd done that because we wanted to help Carrie and Laurence.

Dorothea told Rocky that all the squirrels had fallen silent for a bit and then one said they felt a bit daft for shouting "**SIT!**" at us when we were off to do something so noble, and then another said maybe they should think about helping us, and another said they should maybe work as a team like us dogs. They ended up gathering all the squirrels they could find and went into the room to be transported to the Arctic like us.

They had followed the trail like we had done, but when they saw the houses in the distance they headed towards them instead. These houses were where Father and Mother Christmas lived. They met Mother Christmas and explained what was going on, and she sent a message to FC. She said FC would need help locating us in the snow and that's where the squirrels could help.

They'd searched for us and then formed themselves into an arrow so that FC would know where we were.

So it looks like we'd inspired them to work together and to look out for others, and it ended up helping to save us.

Dad was getting impatient now and kept pulling my lead to get me away from Rocky, which was fair enough as it was Christmas Day and we had presents to unwrap. Presents that FC, after a tip-off from me, had recovered from the cabin and managed to deliver in the nick of time. One of them delivered to our house happened to be bike-shaped...

As we were heading home, sitting on the red

thing on the corner was Dorothea. When I passed, I gave her a nod and she nodded back.

"**Merry Christmas, Dorothea,**" I said. "**Merry Christmas.**"

Acknowledgements

Thanks to Anita, my partner in crime, for doing such a wonderful job with the illustrations. Always a joy. To Lauren Fortune, my editor, for her brilliant guidance and encouragement. To Genevieve Herr, Wendy Shakespeare, Aimee Stewart, Beth Mincher, Camilla Chetty, Lisa Davies and Lucy Bint, and everyone at Scholastic for their help and know-how. To Penelope Daukes for being the best at PR there is. To Paul Stevens, Peter Nixon and everyone who has helped along the way. To my family for putting up with me spending hour after hour in the spare room typing away. And thanks to you for reading my books – I never take it for granted.

Don't miss these laugh-out-loud, brilliantly silly books by Stephen and Anita Mangan!

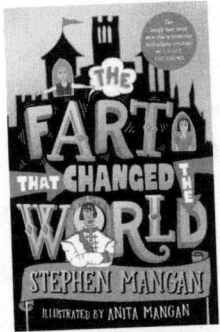